5E MYTHIC CLASSES

All-new character classes
with features from 1ˢᵗ to 20ᵗʰ level

Create the multiverse's mightiest heroes for the world's greatest roleplaying game! With *5e Mythic Classes*, players and Game Masters can now create charismatic shield-throwing warriors, shape-shifting lycanthrope adventurers, and brilliant inventors who craft powerful suits of mechanical armor. Best of all, mythic classes function in exactly the same way as standard classes. You can introduce mythic classes into both ongoing campaigns and brand new adventures, starting at 1ˢᵗ level.

Author: Christopher Brazelton

INTRODUCTION

Standard 5e character classes offer wonderful variety—enough to create almost any character imaginable. Mythic classes increase the range of possibilities even further.

Mythic classes differ from standard classes in their more focused abilities. In general, mythic classes wield more power than standard classes, at the cost of versatility. Each mythic class represents special training, lore, and abilities available only to members of that class. For example, mythic classes master specific weapon types, schools of magic, or fighting styles.

Mythic Classes vs. Prestige Classes

Some tabletop roleplaying games include the concept of "prestige" classes. Mythic classes differ from prestige classes in important respects.

First, any character can choose any mythic class. Many versions of prestige classes require characters to choose specific feats, skill proficiencies, races, ability scores, and class levels before starting prestige class advancement. Mythic classes have primary ability scores like standard classes, but are open to all characters at 1st level.

Second, all mythic classes offer a complete character advancement path from 1st to 20th level. You can choose a mythic class starting at 1st level and learn new abilities over the course of an entire campaign.

Finally, mythic classes feature the full range of customization options accessibly by standard 5e classes. Every mythic class includes two archetypes, starting equipment, and background information to help you create your mythic character.

MYTHIC CLASSES IN YOUR CAMPAIGN

When should you include mythic classes in a campaign? Mythic classes work best in the following scenarios:

New Players. If you plan to run a campaign for players new to 5e (or tabletop roleplaying games in general), consider allowing mythic classes in addition to standard classes. Mythic classes will keep players engaged with new features and options at every level.

1st Level Campaigns. All mythic classes choose an archetype at 1st level, making them ideal for campaigns that begin at 1st level.

Heroic Campaigns. Mythic classes possess more power than non-heroic standard classes. At your Game Master's discretion, you can choose a mythic class instead of a standard class for heroic campaigns.

Superheroes. While some superhero concepts can emerge through careful multiclassing, the process usually takes several levels to complete. Mythic classes adapt abilities of characters from myth and fiction for use in 5e, starting from 1st level.

USING THIS BOOK

Chapter 1 summarizes each mythic class, and explains how to use mythic classes when creating a new character. Chapter 1 also details multiclassing options for mythic classes. Chapters 2-6 provide a complete explanation for each mythic class.

The Appendices contain bonus options for your 5e adventures, such as the first subclass open to two different character classes.

You will need the core rules of 5e (not found in this book) to create and play a character. The classes detailed in *5e Mythic Classes* are compatible with all previous books in the Heroic 5e series.

CHAPTER 1: MYTHIC CLASSES

Standard 5e classes generally represent callings, traditions, or archetypes common among adventurers. Mythic classes offer greater power in more rare and specialized roles. In the same way that few warriors are true fighters or paladins, few adventurers can claim a mythic class.

At your Game Master's discretion, characters can advance in more than one mythic class, or in a combination of standard and mythic class levels. Mythic classes do not have any ability score prerequisites.

Advancement beyond 1st level for mythic characters follows the same experience point progression as standard classes. For example, a defender needs the same 300 experience points to advance from 1st level to 2nd level as any other character.

The Mythic Classes table lists the five mythic classes featured in this book. Some classes represent adaptations of legendary figures—both ancient and modern. Others represent a new interpretation for archetypes that do not currently appear in the 5e core rules.

Mythic Classes

Class	Description	Hit Die	Primary Ability	Saving Throw Proficiencies	Armor and Weapon Proficiencies
Defender	A warrior who uses a shield for both attack and defense	d10	Strength	Strength, Constitution & Charisma	All armor, shields, simple and martial weapons.
Felblade	A spellcaster and warrior who drains vitality from their enemies	d8	Strength & Charisma	Dexterity & Wisdom	Light and medium armor, simple weapons, battleaxes, greataxes, greatswords, longswords
Ferroclad	A brilliant inventor who crafts suits of mechanical armor	d10	Intelligence	Strength & Intelligence	All armor, shields, and simple weapons
Protean	A shapeshifter who uses the power of nature to transform into animal shapes, and animal-humanoid hybrid forms	d12	Charisma	Constitution & Charisma	Shields, simple weapons
Stormcaller	A divine warrior who commands wind, thunder, and lightning	D8	Strength & Wisdom	Wisdom & Charisma	Light armor, simple weapons, mauls, morningstars, warhammers

CHAPTER 2: DEFENDER

A sturdy dwarf hurls her shield at a charging gorgon. The shield scores the gorgon's metallic hide before returning to her hand.

A plate-armored tiefling rallies his comrades, directing them into the perfect positions to repel the assault of an orcish warband. Arrows and javelins strike the tiefling's luminous shield with no effect.

These warriors exemplify the strengths of the defender. A defender's shield serves as both a bastion of hope, and a deadly weapon in the defender's hands. Defenders train their bodies with rigor and discipline, achieving unrivaled mastery of offensive and defensive shield fighting.

IMPENETRABLE DEFENSE

Even an ordinary shield transforms into a formidable magical barrier in the hands of a defender. Defenders undergo rigorous martial trailing, and learn to channel arcane energy through their shields.

Some defenders choose to focus their training on extending this arcane energy, called defender magic, in order to inspire their allies in combat.

SUPERIOR SOLDIERS

Most defenders receive their training as part of professional armies. Veteran defenders choose warriors from among rank-and-file troops, selecting soldiers who display the utmost bravery, combat prowess, and tactical acumen. These hand-picked soldiers learn the secrets of defender magic and combat techniques.

In peaceful times, some defenders choose the life of an adventurer as a means to combat evil and defend civilization. These defenders operate with maximal independence based on the expectation that they will always return to support their comrades. An adventuring defender who recognizes no ongoing obligations may have left military service in defiance of unjust or evil orders.

Defenders function best in small groups of elite warriors, making them ideal adventuring companions.

CREATING A DEFENDER

As you make your defender character, think about why you left military service. Did you leave with the blessing of your fellow defenders, or under questionable circumstances? If you freely chose adventuring, how do you view your obligation to military service?

Due to their highly regimented military training, almost all defenders are of lawful alignment. Defenders rarely turn to evil, but a few have abandoned their noble ideals to pursue selfish or destructive goals.

QUICK BUILD

You can make a defender quickly by following these suggestions. First, make Strength your highest ability score, followed by Constitution. Second, choose the soldier background.

The Defender – Class Table

Level	Proficiency Bonus	Features
1st	+2	Shield Throw, Defender Archetype
2nd	+2	Fighting Style, Marvelous Body
3rd	+2	Defender Archetype Feature
4th	+2	Ability Score Improvement
5th	+3	Extra Attack
6th	+3	Mythic Endurance (two uses), Evasion
7th	+3	Defender Archetype Feature
8th	+3	Ability Score Improvement
9th	+4	Battle Tactics
10th	+4	Defender Archetype Feature
11th	+4	Flawless Body
12th	+4	Ability Score Improvement
13th	+5	Extra Attack (2)
14th	+5	Guardian Barrier
15th	+5	Defender Archetype Feature
16th	+5	Ability Score Improvement
17th	+6	Mythic Endurance (three uses)
18th	+6	Inexhaustible Vitality
19th	+6	Ability Score Improvement
20th	+6	Defender Archetype Feature

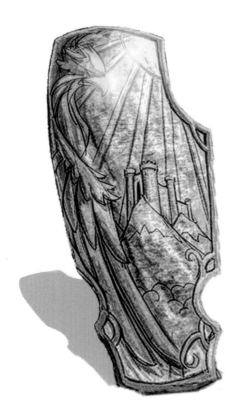

Class Features

As a defender, you gain the following features.

Hit Points

Hit Dice: 1d10 per defender level
Hit Points at 1st Level: 10 + your Constitution modifier
Hit Points at Higher Levels: 1d10 (or 6) + your Constitution modifier per defender level after 1st

Proficiencies

Armor: All armor, shields
Weapons: Simple weapons, martial weapons
Tools: None

Saving Throws: Strength, Constitution, Charisma
Skills: Choose three skills from Acrobatics, Arcana, Athletics, Insight, Intimidation, Perception, Persuasion, and Survival

Equipment

You start with the following equipment, in addition to the equipment granted by your background:

- (*a*) chain mail or (*b*) studded leather
- (*a*) a martial weapon and a shield or (*b*) two simple weapons and a shield
- (*a*) a light crossbow and 20 bolts or (*b*) two handaxes
- (*a*) a dungeoneer's pack or (*b*) an explorer's pack

Defender Archetype

At 1st level, you choose an archetype that guides your use of defender magic and shield fighting. Choose either Shield Warden or Field Commander, both of which are detailed at the end of the class description. The archetype you choose grants you features at 1st level and again at 3rd, 7th, 10th, 15th, and 20th level.

Defender Magic

Defender magic resembles the spells learned by other arcane spellcasters. However, defenders only share their knowledge with warriors whom they judge worthy. Any warrior with an aptitude for magical study can learn defender magic, provided that they find a defender willing to instruct them.

Some of your defender features require your target to make a saving throw to resist the feature's effects. The saving throw DC is calculated as follows:

Defender save DC
= 8 + your proficiency bonus + your Strength modifier

Shield Fighting

At 1st level, your defender training gives you mastery of combat styles that use a shield both for protection and as a weapon. You gain the following benefits while you are wielding a shield:

- Shields are considered one-handed martial melee weapons for you that deal 1d8 bludgeoning damage.
- If the shield is magical and grants a bonus to AC in addition to the shield's normal AC, you may add that bonus to attack and damage rolls made with the shield. For example, a *shield +1* would grant a +1 bonus to attack and damage rolls you make with the *shield +1*.
- When you use the Attack action with a shield on your turn, you can make one unarmed strike as a bonus action. You can roll a d4 in place of the normal damage of your unarmed strike. This die changes when you reach certain levels in this class: 5th level (d6), 11th level (d8) and 17th level (d10)
- When another creature would hit you with a weapon attack or a spell that requires an attack roll, you can use your reaction to add 5 to your AC against the attack. To do so, you must see the attacker.

Shield Throw

At 1st level, you know the defender techniques for throwing a shield to make ranged attacks. Shields have the thrown property for you, with a normal range of 30 feet, and a long range of 80 feet.

When you are wielding a shield, you can use the Attack action to throw the shield. Strength is your ability modifier for the attack and damage rolls. Immediately after the attack, the shield flies back to your hand. Your defender magic guides the shield, returning the shield to your hand even if the attack misses.

Improvised Shield Throwing

The 5e core rules allow for the use of objects, and melee weapons that do not have the thrown property, as improvised thrown weapons at the Game Master's discretion. Defenders have mastered shield throwing, but your Game Master might allow other characters to use shields as improvised thrown weapons. A ranged weapon attack made using a shield as an improvised weapon deals 1d4 bludgeoning damage, with a normal range of 20 feet and a long range of 60 feet.

At the Game Master's option, a character proficient with shields can add their proficiency bonus to the attack roll when making a ranged weapon attack using a shield.

FIGHTING STYLE

At 2nd level, you adopt a style of fighting as your specialty. Choose one of the following options. You can't take a Fighting Style option more than once, even if you later get to choose again.

DEFENSE

While you are wearing armor, you gain a +1 bonus to AC.

DUELING

When you are wielding a melee weapon in one hand and no other weapons, you gain a +2 bonus to damage rolls with that weapon. You still gain this bonus when you are wielding a shield, but you cannot add this bonus to damage rolls made with a shield.

PROTECTION

When a creature you can see attacks a target other than you that is within 5 feet of you, you can use your reaction to impose disadvantage on the attack roll. You must be wielding a shield.

RETALIATION

When a creature within 5 feet of you attacks a target other than you, you can use your reaction to make a melee weapon attack against the attacker.

MARVELOUS BODY

At 2nd level, your defender training allows you to move and act more quickly. You can take a bonus action on each of your turns in combat. This action can be used only to take the Dash, Disengage, or Help action.

ABILITY SCORE IMPROVEMENT

When you reach 4th level, and again at 8th, 12th, 16th, and 19th level, you can increase one ability score of your choice by 2, or you can increase two ability scores of your choice by 1.

If you are using options from *5e Legendary Heroes* to create a heroic character, you can increase an ability score up to a maximum of 30. Otherwise, you can't increase an ability score above 20 using this feature.

EXTRA ATTACK

Beginning at 5th level, you can attack twice, instead of once, whenever you take the Attack action on your turn. The number of attacks increases to three when you reach 13th level in this class.

EVASION

At 6th level, your combat experience and agility let you dodge out of the way of certain area effects, such as a black dragon's caustic breath or a *flame strike* spell. When you are subjected to an effect that allows you to make a Dexterity saving throw to take only half damage, you instead take no damage if you succeed on the saving throw, and only half damage if you fail.

MYTHIC ENDURANCE

Starting at 6th level, the arcane energy that enhances your shield fortifies your body. You can expend a use of this feature to gain one of the following effects:

- When a creature scores a critical hit on an attack that targets only you, you can force the attack to deal normal damage. For example, a creature that scores a critical hit against you using a greataxe would only roll 1d12 for the damage, rather than 2d12, and then add the relevant ability modifier.
- When you are reduced to 0 hit points but not killed outright, you can make a DC 15

Constitution saving throw. On a success, you can drop to 1 hit point instead.
- You have resistance to bludgeoning, piercing, and slashing damage until the end of your next turn.

You have two uses of this feature at 6th level, and you gain one additional use at 17th level. You regain all expended uses when you finish a long rest. You can use this feature only once on the same turn.

BATTLE TACTICS

By 9th level, your reflexes and threat assessment faculties are so keen that you have advantage on initiative rolls.

In addition, you can use a bonus action on each of your turns to maneuver one of your allies into a more advantageous position. Choose a friendly creature who can see or hear you. That creature can use its reaction to move up to half its speed without provoking opportunity attacks.

FLAWLESS BODY

At 11th level, the arcane energy that fuels your defender powers makes you immune to disease and poison.

GUARDIAN BARRIER

Starting at 14th level, you can channel energy to make your shield an impenetrable barrier. You can use an action to make yourself immune to nonmagical damage until the end of your next turn. Once you use this feature, you must finish a long rest before you can use it again.

INEXHAUSTIBLE VITALITY

At 18th level, the arcane energy that infuses your body grants you advantage on death saving throws. In addition, whenever you roll a Hit Die to regain hit points, double the number of hit points it restores.

DEFENDER ARCHETYPES

Defender training teaches a balanced approach that includes combat techniques and magical study. Defenders then choose to focus on a particular aspect of their training, represented by the Shield Warden and Field Commander archetypes.

SHIELD WARDEN

Shield Wardens emphasize perfection of shield fighting, and practice defender magic that imbues their shield attacks with arcane energy.

IMPROVED BLOCK

Beginning when you choose this archetype at 1st level, you can quickly counterattack when you block a foe's attack with your shield. When a creature misses you with a melee attack, you can make one melee weapon attack against it using your reaction.

You can make this special attack even if you have already expended your reaction this turn, but only once each round.

IMPROVED SHIELD FIGHTING

By 3rd level, you have developed a powerful shield combat style. You gain one of the following features of your choice.

Shield Charge. You learn to set your shield for a devastating ramming attack. If you move at least 20 feet straight toward a target and then hit it with a shield attack on the same turn, the target takes an extra 1d8 bludgeoning damage. When you reach 14th level, the extra damage increases to 2d8.

If the target is no more than one size larger than you, it must succeed on a Strength saving throw or be knocked prone.

Shield Ricochet. You master the ability to direct the path of your shield to strike multiple foes. Once on each of your turns when you use your Shield Throw feature, you can make another Shield Throw attack against a different creature within 5 feet of the original target and within range of your Shield Throw. The shield returns to your hand immediately after the second attack.

The number of additional targets increases to 2 when you reach 14th level in this class. You can make the third Shield Throw attack against a different creature (including the first Shield Throw's target as a valid target) within 5 feet of the second target and within range of your Shield Throw. The shield returns to your hand immediately after the third attack.

WARDEN SHIELD: ATTRACTION

At 7th level, you can use a bonus action to enchant your shield to attract projectiles for 1 minute. While holding the shield, you have resistance to damage from ranged weapon attacks.

Whenever a ranged weapon attack is made against a target within 10 feet of you, you can use your reaction to become the attack's target instead. You gain a +2 bonus to AC against the attack.

Once this feature's effect ends, you cannot use it again for 1 minute. The effect ends immediately if you are incapacitated, or if you use another Warden Shield feature.

SHIELD BASH

Beginning at 10th level, you can channel a burst of concussive force through your shield. When you hit another creature with a melee weapon attack using a shield, you can attempt a shield bash. The target must succeed on a Constitution saving throw or be stunned until the end of your next turn.

You can use this feature a number of times equal to 1 + your Strength modifier (a minimum of twice). When you finish a long rest, you regain all expended uses.

WARDEN SHIELD: REFLECTION

Starting at 15th level, you can use a bonus action to enchant your shield to resist and repel magical effects for 1 minute. While holding the shield, you have advantage on saving throws against spells and other magical effects, and spell attacks have disadvantage against you.

When you are targeted by a *magic missile* spell, or a spell that requires a ranged attack roll, you can use your reaction and roll a d6. On a 5 or 6, you are unaffected, and the effect is reflected back at the caster as though it originated from you, turning the caster into the target.

Once this feature's effect ends, you cannot use it again for 1 minute. The effect ends immediately if you are incapacitated, or if you use another Warden Shield feature.

WARDEN SHIELD: REVENGE

At 20th level, you can use a bonus action to enchant your shield to absorb damage for 1 minute. While holding the shield, you can use your reaction when another creature hits you with a melee or ranged attack, and when a hostile creature casts a spell of 5th level or lower that targets only you. If you do, your shield absorbs the damage and any harmful effects, and gains 1 charge.

Once on each of your turns when you make a melee weapon attack, you can expend 1 charge to deal an additional 5d8 force damage, in addition to the weapon's damage. You have advantage on the attack roll if the creature has hit you with an attack or harmful spell within the last minute.

Once this feature's effect ends, your shield loses all charges, and you must finish a short or long rest before you can use it again. The effect ends immediately if you are incapacitated, or if you use another Warden Shield feature.

FIELD COMMANDER

Defenders who guide their training based on the archetypal Field Commander study defender magic that strengthens both themselves and their allies.

GUARDIAN AURA

When you choose this archetype at 1st level, you learn to extend the magic that emanates from your shield to protect your allies. At the start of your turn while you are wielding a shield, you and friendly creatures within 10 feet of you gain 1d4 temporary hit points.

The temporary hit points granted by this feature increase when you reach certain levels in this class: 7th level (2d4), 14th level (3d4), and 19th level (4d4). When you reach 18th level, the range of this aura increases to 30 feet.

BATTLEFIELD UNITY

Beginning at 3rd level, you can empower your Guardian Aura to radiate arcane energy that intensifies with the support of your allies. You gain one of the following features of your choice:

Shield Wall. Spectral shields surround your allies and protect them from harm. Friendly creatures within the range of your Guardian Aura can use their reaction to gain a +1 bonus to AC against one melee attack that would hit them.

This AC bonus increase to +2 when two or more friendly creatures are within the range of your Guardian Aura.

Thorns. When a creature hits you or a friendly creature within the range of your Guardian Aura with a melee attack, the attacker takes 1d4 piercing damage.

The damage increases to 2d4 when two or more friendly creatures are within the range of your Guardian Aura.

Aura of Might

By 7th level, your inspiring leadership and defender magic guides and augments attacks. You and friendly creatures within range of your Guardian Aura can add your Charisma modifier (a minimum of +1) to all attack and damage rolls.

Commander's Shield

At 10th level, you can channel arcane energy into your shield strikes. Once on each of your turns when you hit a creature with a melee weapon attack, you can cause the attack to deal an additional 1d6 force damage to the target. When you reach 14th level, the extra damage increases to 2d6. In addition, you gain one of the following features of your choice:

Commander's Mark. You learn to infuse your shield with arcane energy that exposes gaps in a foe's defenses. When you hit a creature with a weapon attack using your shield, you can use a bonus action to mark the target until the end of your next turn.

The next attack roll against a marked target by an attacker other than you has advantage. On a hit, the attack deals an additional 1d6 force damage.

Disabling Strike. You learn to charge your shield with arcane energy that weakens foes. When you hit a creature with a weapon attack using a shield, you can use a bonus action to release the shield's energy into the target. The target must make a Constitution saving throw.

On a failed save, the target's speed is halved and it can't take reactions until the end of your next turn. The target deals only half damage with attacks that use Strength until the end of your next turn.

Aura of Fortification

Starting at 15th level, your Guardian Aura conceals and protects your allies. You and friendly creatures within the range of your Guardian Aura can't be targeted by any divination magic or perceived through magical scrying sensors.

When a hostile creature attempts to enter the area of your Guardian Aura for the first time on a turn or starts its turn there, it must make a Wisdom saving throw. On a failed save, the aura repels the creature. The creature cannot willingly move closer to you or any friendly creatures within the aura.

At the end of each of the creature's turns, it can make a Wisdom saving throw to resist the aura's repulsion, ending the effect on itself on a success. If a creature succeeds on the saving throw, it is immune to the aura's repelling effect for 1 hour.

Aura of Triumph

Beginning at 20th level, allies within your Guardian Aura feel an unshakeable certainty of impending victory. You and allies within your Guardian Aura can reroll one failed saving throw each turn, and must use the new result.

You and friendly creatures within the range of your Guardian Aura can't be charmed or frightened. If a friendly creature is charmed or frightened when they enter the aura, the effect is suspended while they remain within the aura.

CHAPTER 3: FELBLADE

Wielding a greataxe etched with glowing runes, a wounded human beheads a fleeing goblin scout. The runes flare with vivid green light as the human's injuries rapidly mend and disappear.

As night falls, a young halfling strides toward an assassin crouching in the shadows outside her lord's bedroom window. Ghostly hands emerge from the wall, seizing the assassin while the halfling readies her greatsword to strike a killing blow.

Felblades favor an aggressive fighting style that relies on proficiency with two-handed weapons. Against particularly dangerous opponents, felblades can call upon terrible curses to ensure victory.

CURSE BRINGERS

Felblades devote themselves to eradicating evil while drawing power from the evil creatures that they slay.

To amplify their abilities and protect themselves from the corrupting influence of evil, felblades channel their powers through ritually enchanted weapons, called felblades. Therefore, "felblade" refers both to an individual, and to their signature weapon.

SECRET RITES

Felblades gather in secretive orders to study spells that inflict pain, and to practice great weapon fighting techniques. Felblade orders teach differing rites that tend to emphasize either mastery of great weapon fighting, or shaping the soul and psyche to conjure a spectral ally.

A felblade order rarely has more than twenty members at any time. Most felblades choose to hunt evil alone, or in small adventuring parties. Some orders pledge loyalty to gods of goodness and justice. Others share a bond based on belief in ideals of goodness reinforced by a grim hatred of evil.

Felblades might not adventure to acquire wealth, but their steadfast opposition to dangerous evil creatures makes them invaluable adventuring companions.

The Felblade – Class Table

Level	Proficiency Bonus	Features	Spell Slots per Spell Level 1st	2nd	3rd	4th	5th
1st	+2	Spellcasting, Felblade Order, Infuse Blade	2	-	-	-	-
2nd	+2	Fighting Style	2	-	-	-	-
3rd	+2	Felblade Order Feature, Summon Weapon	3	-	-	-	-
4th	+2	Ability Score Improvement	3	-	-	-	-
5th	+3	Extra Attack	4	2	-	-	-
6th	+3	Bind Soul	4	2	-		
7th	+3	Felblade Order Feature	4	3	-	-	-
8th	+3	Ability Score Improvement	4	3	-		
9th	+4	Sentient Weapon	4	3	2	-	-
10th	+4	Felblade Order Feature	4	3			
11th	+4	Drain Soul,	4	3	3	-	-
12th	+4	Ability Score Improvement	4	3			
13th	+5	Sunder Soul	4	3	3	1	-
14th	+5	Felblade Order Feature	4	3			
15th	+5	Grim Channeling	4	3	3	2	-
16th	+5	Ability Score Improvement	4	3			
17th	+6	Consume Soul	4	3	3	3	1
18th	+6	Felblade Order Feature	4	3			
19th	+6	Ability Score Improvement	4	3	3	3	2
20th	+6	Soul Mastery	4	3			

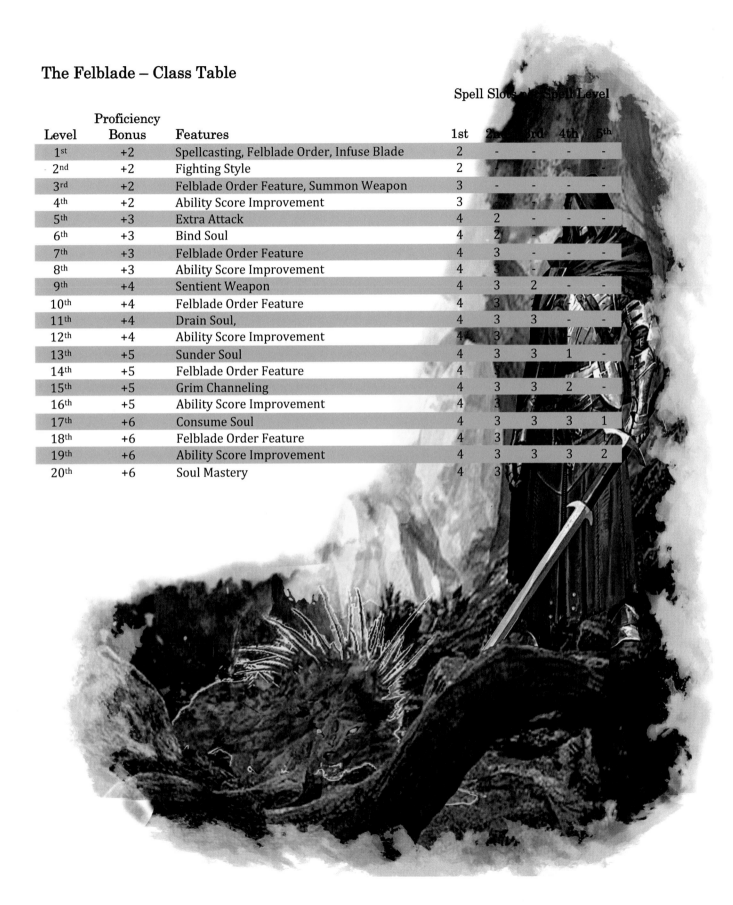

CREATING A FELBLADE

As you make your felblade character, think about what drives you to fight evil. Does your order specialize in combating a particular type of evil creature? Did a fiend, vampire, or evil dragon kill someone close to you? Do you seek revenge against a specific evil creature, or adventure as a means to exterminate evil in all of its forms?

Next, think about the principles that guide your felblade order. Did you receive training from an order that worships a good deity? If so, do you have any connection with clerics and paladins who worship the same deity? The rigid and often fanatical mindset of felblade orders sometimes places them at odds with other divine warriors.

Almost all felblades lean towards a lawful or chaotic good alignment, but a few felblades become corrupted by their exposure to wickedness. Evil felblades find themselves hunted both by other felblades and by the evil creatures they once pursued.

QUICK BUILD

You can make a felblade quickly by following these suggestions. First, Strength should be your highest ability score, followed by Charisma. Second, choose the hermit background.

CLASS FEATURES

As a felblade, you gain the following class features.

HIT POINTS

Hit Dice: 1d8 per felblade level
Hit Points at 1st Level: 8 + your Constitution modifier
Hit Points at Higher Levels: 1d8 (or 5) + your Constitution modifier per felblade level after 1st

PROFICIENCIES

Armor: Light armor, medium armor
Weapons: Simple weapons, battleaxes, greataxes, greatswords, longswords
Tools: None

Saving Throws: Dexterity, Wisdom

Skills: Choose two from Arcana, Athletics, Insight, Intimidation, Investigation, Perception, and Religion

EQUIPMENT

You start with the following equipment, in addition to the equipment granted by your background:

- (a) scale mail, (b) studded leather armor, or (c) chain mail (if proficient)
- (a) a battleaxe, (b) greataxe, (c) greatsword, or (d) longsword
- (a) a light crossbow and 20 bolts or (b) any simple weapon
- (a) a dungeoneer's pack or (b) a priest's pack

SPELLCASTING

Your training in felblade rites gives you the ability to cast spells. Felblade orders teach an ancient form of divine spellcasting with a focus on spells that injure or weaken foes.

PREPARING AND CASTING SPELLS

The Felblade table shows how many spell slots you have to cast your spells. To cast one of your felblade spells of 1st level or higher, you must expend a spell slot of the spell's level or higher. You regain all expended spell slots when you finish a long rest.

You prepare the list of felblade spells that are available for you to cast, choosing from the felblade spell list at the end of this chapter. When you do so, choose a number of felblade spells equal to your Charisma modifier + your felblade level (minimum of one spell). The spells must be of a level for which you have spell slots.

For example, if you are a 9th level felblade, you have four 1st-level, three 2nd-level, and two 3rd-level spell slots. With a Charisma modifier of 16, your list of prepared spells could include seven spells of 1st, 2nd, or 3rd level, in any combination. If you prepare the 1st-level spell *inflict wounds*, you can cast it using a 1st, 2nd, or 3rd-level slot. Casting the spell does not remove it from your list of prepared spells.

You can change your list of prepared spells when you finish a long rest. Preparing a new list of felblade spells requires time spent in meditation, at least 1 minute per spell level for each spell on your list.

SPELLCASTING ABILITY

Charisma is your spellcasting ability for your felblade spells, since the power flows from the strength of your convictions. You use your Charisma whenever a spell refers to your spellcasting ability. In addition, you use your Charisma modifier when setting the saving throw DC for a felblade spell you cast and when making an attack roll with one.

Felblade spell save DC
= 8 + your proficiency bonus + your Charisma modifier

Spell attack modifier
= 8 + your proficiency bonus + your Charisma modifier

SPELLCASTING FOCUS

You can use your felblade weapon as a spellcasting focus for your felblade spells.

IMPROVED HEX

As a felblade, your order training gives you facility with curses. Beginning at 1st level, you always have the *hex* spell prepared, and it doesn't count against the number of spells you can prepare each day.

In addition, you can use a bonus action on each of your turns to cast *hex* at 1st level without expending a spell slot and without material components. You must still maintain concentration in order to keep the spell active.

FELBLADE ORDER

At 1st level, choose a felblade order: Inquisitor or Dread Hunter, both of which are detailed at the end of the class description. Your choice grants you features at 1st level and again at 3rd, 7th, 10th, 14th, and 18th level.

Felblades pass on their knowledge in small groups of like-minded warriors, called orders. Your felblade order selection represents the prevailing philosophy and teachings of the felblade order in which you received your early training.

INFUSE BLADE

By 1st level, you have learned the felblade rites to create a magical bond with one weapon. This bond transforms the weapon into a felblade (hereafter referred to as a "felblade weapon" or "bonded weapon" for the sake of clarity). Bonding to a nonmagical weapon using this feature does not count towards the maximum number of magic items you can be attuned to at a time.

You must be proficient with the weapon in order to form this bond. You perform the rites over the course of 1 hour, which can take place during a short rest. The weapon must be within your reach throughout the ritual, at the conclusion of which you touch the weapon to forge the bond.

While you wield the felblade weapon, you gain the following benefits:

- Your attacks made with the weapon are considered magical for the purpose of overcoming resistance and immunity to nonmagical attacks and damage
- You can perform the somatic components of spells even when you have the weapon in one or both hands
- You can't be disarmed of the weapon unless you are incapacitated

Most bonded weapons show some permanent visible change at the conclusion of the bonding rites, such as glowing script (in a language spoken by the weapon's wielder), an aura of dim light, or an altered surface material (e.g., bronze, silver, or obsidian). You choose the weapon's new appearance, but your Game Master has the final say on whether the weapon's appearance is appropriate for the campaign setting.

You can bond to one weapon at a time. You can perform the rites to break the bond and bond with a new weapon over the course of a short rest.

FIGHTING STYLE

At 2nd level, you adopt a style of fighting as your specialty. Choose one of the following options. You can't take a Fighting Style option more than once, even if you later get to choose again.

DUELING

When you are wielding a melee weapon in one hand and no other weapons, you gain a +2 bonus to damage rolls with that weapon.

EXECUTIONER

You gain a +2 bonus to melee weapon attack rolls you make against any creature that doesn't have all of its hit points.

GREAT WEAPON FIGHTING

When you roll a 1 or 2 on a damage die for an attack you make with a melee weapon that you are wielding with two hands, you can reroll the die and must use the new roll, even if the new roll is a 1 or a 2. The weapon must have the two-handed or versatile property for you to gain this benefit.

TWO-WEAPON FIGHTING

When you engage in two-weapon fighting, you can add your ability modifier to the damage roll of the second attack. Felblades who practice two-weapon fighting typically reserve any killing blow for their felblade weapon.

SUMMON WEAPON

Starting at 3rd level, the bond with your felblade weapon allows you to call the weapon to your hand. If your felblade weapon is on the same plane of existence, you can summon that weapon as a bonus action on your turn, causing it to teleport instantly to your hand.

If your felblade weapon is on a different plane of existence, you can summon that weapon as a bonus action on your turn. The weapon teleports to your hand at the start of your next turn.

ABILITY SCORE IMPROVEMENT

When you reach 4th level, and again at 8th, 12th, 16th, and 19th level, you can increase one ability score of your choice by 2, or you can increase two ability scores of your choice by 1.

If you are using options from *5e Legendary Heroes* to create a heroic character, you can increase an ability score up to a maximum of 30. Otherwise, you can't increase an ability score above 20 using this feature.

EXTRA ATTACK

Beginning at 5th level, you can attack twice, instead of once, whenever you take the Attack action on your turn.

BIND SOUL

Starting at 6th level, the bond with your felblade weapon anchors your soul. If you die while wielding your felblade weapon, your soul enters the weapon. You can remain in the weapon or depart for the afterlife. As long as your soul is in the weapon, you can telepathically communicate with any creature who touches it.

While your soul remains in the weapon, if a spell would have the sole effect of restoring you to life (but not undeath), the caster does not need material components to cast the spell on you.

SENTIENT WEAPON

By 9th level, your study of felblade rites enables you to manifest sentience in your felblade weapon.

You perform the rites over the course of 8 hours, which can take place during a long rest. The weapon must be within your reach throughout the ritual, at the conclusion of which you touch the weapon to awaken its sentience.

The weapon shares your alignment and goals, with an Intelligence of 10, a Wisdom of 10, and a Charisma of 12. It has hearing and darkvision out to a range of 120 feet.

The weapon can read and understand all languages you know, and can communicate with you telepathically.

Sentient weapons created by felblades develop personalities similar to their wielder. However, the weapon communicates as an NPC under the Game Master's control.

DRAIN SOUL

At 11th level, your felblade weapon can siphon the souls of slain creatures. When you reduce a creature to 0 hit points with a weapon attack using your felblade weapon, the target immediately dies, and can't become undead or return to life via magical means for 24 hours unless you allow it.

Residual energy from the creature's soul empowers you. For 1 minute, you can add your Charisma modifier to weapon damage rolls made for your felblade weapon.

SUNDER SOUL

Beginning at 13th level, your felblade weapon attacks can temporarily weaken foes. When you hit a hostile creature with a melee weapon attack using your felblade weapon, you can use a bonus action to sunder the target's soul. The creature has disadvantage on all saving throws until the end of your next turn. In addition, the next attack made against the creature before the end of your next turn has advantage.

Once you use this feature, you cannot use it again for 1 minute.

GRIM CHANNELING

Starting at 15th level when you cast a felblade spell of 1st level or higher, you can contribute a portion of your own vitality to increase the spell's level.

If you do, you suffer 1d8 necrotic damage per additional spell level, up to a maximum of 4d8. This damage cannot be reduced by any means, and your hit point maximum is reduced by an amount equal to the necrotic damage dealt until you finish a long rest. You can increase a spell's effective level beyond your maximum spell slot level using this feature.

If a spell requires an attack roll, you can choose to suffer the necrotic damage before or after making the attack roll, but before any effects of the spell are applied.

For example, if you cast *inflict wounds* using a 1st-level spell slot, you could choose to suffer 1d8 necrotic damage and treat the spell as if it were cast using a 2nd-level spell slot, increasing the spell's damage by 1d10.

CONSUME SOUL

By 17th level, you have such mastery over your felblade weapon that you can use it to temporarily capture the souls of your enemies, and heal your wounds.

When you reduce a hostile creature to 0 hit points, you can force the creature to make a Charisma saving throw. On a failed save, you trap the creature's soul in your felblade weapon, and you regain hit points equal to five times your felblade level.

Once you regain hit points using this feature, you cannot use it again until you finish a long rest. The trapped soul moves on to the afterlife at the end of your next long rest.

SOUL MASTERY

At 20th level, your expertise in felblade rites and the bond with your felblade weapon have deepened so much that you have immunity to radiant and necrotic damage.

When a creature dies while affected by a spell you cast of 1st level or higher, you can roll a d6. You regain one spell slot with a level equal to the roll. On a roll of 6, you regain one 5th-level spell slot and may roll again.

You can regain spell slots using this feature a number of times equal to your Charisma modifier (a minimum of once). You regain all expended uses at the end of a long rest.

FELBLADE ORDERS

Two traditions predominate among felblade orders. A felblade order teaches only one tradition, shared by all of its members. Felblades continue to improve their abilities, according to their order's foundational teachings, as they defeat evil creatures and strengthen the bond with their felblade weapon.

Felblades who champion different orders view their counterparts as allies, provided that they do not hinder one another in the pursuit of goodness and justice.

ORDER OF THE INQUISITOR

Felblades inducted into the Order of the Inquisitor hold that evil most fears direct and uncompromising engagements. Inquisitor orders may worship good-aligned gods who also preside over war and battle.

BONUS PROFICIENCIES

When you choose this order at 1st level, you gain proficiency with heavy armor and with the Investigation skill. You can add double your proficiency bonus to any Intelligence (Investigation) checks made to detect evil creatures or to analyze their activities.

Manifest Judgment

Also starting at 1st level, you automatically succeed on Constitution saving throws that you make to maintain your concentration on a spell when you take damage, but only if that damage was caused by a creature currently affected by a spell you cast of 1st level or higher.

Rebuke the Deceiver

Beginning at 3rd level, you can call upon a curse to afflict creatures who lie to you. When you succeed on a Wisdom (Insight) check to uncover a creature's lie, you can use a bonus action to curse the creature for 1 minute.

Until the curse ends, the creature can't speak a deliberate lie. In addition, the creature must truthfully answer any questions asked by you to the best of its ability. Once you use this feature, you cannot use it again until the finish a short or long rest.

Felblade Strike

At 7th level, you gain one of the following features of your choice:

Soul Rend. Your felblade weapon cuts through both flesh and spirit. When you hit a creature with a melee weapon attack using your felblade weapon, you can use a bonus action to deal 1d8 psychic damage to the creature.

Cleave. Once on each of your turns when you make a melee weapon attack using your felblade weapon, you can make another attack with your felblade weapon against a different creature that is within 5 feet of the original target and within range of your felblade weapon.

Anointed Weapon

By 10th level, you have learned a ritual to sanctify your felblade weapon and bestow it with additional magical properties.

The ritual costs 25 gp in rare oils and incense. You perform the ritual over the course of 1 hour, which can be done during a short rest. The weapon must be within your reach throughout the ritual, at the conclusion of which you touch the weapon. The weapon gains one of the following effects of your choice:

Holy Weapon. Your felblade weapon deals an additional 2d6 radiant damage to fiends and undead.

Inspired Strikes. Your felblade weapon guides your attacks. Whenever you make an attack roll with your felblade weapon, you can choose to roll an additional d20. You can choose to use this feature after you roll the die, but before the outcome is determined. You choose which of the d20s is used for the attack roll. You can use this feature a number of times equal to your Charisma modifier (a minimum of once), and you regain all expended uses at the end of a long rest.

Consecrated Weapon. The bond with your felblade weapon reinforces your resolve. You can't be charmed or frightened while you wield your felblade weapon.

You can choose to replace this feature's effect with a different one by performing the ritual again over the course of 1 hour, and spending another 25 gp in rare oils and incense.

Curse of Reckoning

Beginning at 14th level, your felblade weapon attacks can drain life from your foes to heal your comrades. Once on each of your turns when you make a melee weapon attack using your felblade, you can use a bonus action to cause a friendly creature within 30 feet of you to regain hit points equal to your felblade level.

Punishing Glare

Starting at 18th level, you can invoke a curse that torments creatures with searing light fueled by their evil deeds. As an action, you can fix your gaze on a creature within 5 feet, and make a melee spell attack roll against the creature.

On a hit, your eyes emit bright light in a 15-foot cone until the end of your turn, and the target takes 10d10 radiant damage. If the creature has an evil alignment, it instead takes 20d10 radiant damage and is blinded for 1 minute.

This damage ignores resistance and immunity, and can't be reduced or avoided by any means. An evil-aligned creature reduced to 0 hit points by this damage disappears in a blinding flash and is destroyed, leaving its possessions behind.

Once you deal radiant damage using this feature, you can't use it again until you finish a long rest.

ORDER OF THE DREAD HUNTER

Dread Hunters conjure spectral companions to aid them in tracking, subduing, and dispatching evil creatures. The spectral companions summoned by Dread Hunters are not undead, but extensions of the felblade's own soul. Dread Hunters view evil creatures as prey and often work as bounty hunters.

SPECTRAL COMPANION

Beginning when you choose this order at 1st level, you use a fragment of your soul to create an incorporeal companion. You can communicate with your companion telepathically and perceive through its senses as long as you are on the same plane of existence.

Your companion has the following properties:

- It is a Medium celestial with an armor class, alignment, proficiency bonus, and ability scores identical to yours
- Its hit point maximum is equal to half of your hit point maximum
- It has a flying speed equal to your walking speed, and can hover
- It has resistance to acid, cold, fire, lightning, thunder, bludgeoning, piercing, and slashing damage from nonmagical weapons
- It can't be charmed, exhausted, grappled paralyzed, petrified, poisoned, prone, or restrained
- It has darkvision with a range of 60 feet
- It understands the languages you speak, but it can't speak
- It can move through other creatures and objects as if they were difficult terrain
- It can hold, carry, and interact with physical objects

If the companion is reduced to 0 hit points, it disappears, and emerges from your body again at the end of your next long rest. As an action, you can temporarily dismiss your companion. It disappears into your felblade weapon where it awaits your summons.

SPECTRAL COMPANION APPEARANCE

The spectral companion's size is Medium, but it can look however you like. Spectral companions most often appear as ghostly reflections of their creators, or take the form of animals such as dogs, birds, or wolves.

You can roll on the following table to determine your spectral companion's form, or use the suggestions to create your own.

D10	Form
1	Humanoid (resembling its creator)
2	Dog
3	Panther
4	Bear
5	Bird (e.g., Owl, Hawk, Eagle)
6	Snake
7	Spider
8	Skeleton (humanoid)
9	Wolf
10	Angel (deva)

You can roll on the following table to determine the substance that most resembles your companion's incorporeal form, or choose one of your own. You might decide that your companion's appearance remains stable over time, or that its appearance changes based on your experiences and mood.

D8	Substance
1	Glass
2	Smoke
3	Gelatin/Slime
4	Sand/Dust Cloud
5	Flame
6	Fog
7	Insect Swarm
8	None (Barely Visible)

Spectral Companion Actions

The companion always obeys your commands. In combat, it rolls its own initiative. You decide what action the companion will take, and where it moves during its turn. Alternatively, you can issue a general command, such as to follow a creature or guard a wounded comrade. If you issue no commands, the companion will defend you and itself against hostile creatures.

As an action, your spectral companion can become invisible. However, anything that it is wearing or carrying remains visible. It can become visible again as a bonus action on its turn.

The companion can use the Attack action on its turn to make one melee attack, using its fists, claws, teeth, or a spectral version of your felblade weapon, as appropriate for its form. On a hit, this attack deals 1d6 radiant or necrotic damage (your choice).

The attack's damage increases by when 1d6 when you reach 6th level (2d6), and again at 13th level (3d6).

Spectral Snare

At 3rd level, your spectral companion can aid your hunt for evil by hindering a foe's escape. Hostile creatures who move within 5 feet of your spectral companion or who start their turn there are slowed. Their movement speed is halved until the end of their next turn, and opportunity attacks made against the slowed creatures have advantage until the end of their next turn.

Curse of Dread

Starting at 7th level, you can use an action to afflict a hostile creature within 30 feet of you with crippling fear. This curse has the following effects on its target:

- You and your spectral companion can sense the target's presence within a 1-mile radius. The curse reveals the target's general direction and distance (but not its exact location) from you.
- Melee attacks made against the target by your or your spectral companion deal an additional 1d6 psychic damage
- The target must succeed on a Wisdom saving throw to move within 60 feet of you

or your spectral companion. On a failed save, the target becomes frightened for 1 minute. The target can repeat this saving throw at the end of each of its turns. On a success, the target is no longer frightened, and is immune to this effect of the curse for 1 hour.

The curse afflicts the target until you use an action to target a different creature with your Curse of Dread. A *remove curse* spell also ends this feature's effects.

Spectral Form

By 10th level, you have learned to assume an incorporeal form. As an action, you can shift into a spectral form, gaining the following benefits:

- You gain a flying speed equal to your walking speed
- You can move through other creatures and objects as if they were difficult terrain
- You can use a bonus action on your turn to become invisible. You reappear if you attack or cast a spell.
- You can't be grappled, knocked prone, or restrained

This effect ends if you are reduced to 0 hit points, after 1 hour, or if you choose to end it again as a bonus action. If you occupy the same spot as a solid object or creature when this happens, you are immediately shunted to the nearest unoccupied space that you can occupy and take force damage equal to twice the number of feet you are moved.

Once you return to your corporeal form, you cannot use this feature again until you finish a short or long rest.

Dread Specter

Beginning at 14th level, you can perform a ritual to empower your spectral companion. The ritual costs 25 gp in rare oils and incense. You perform the ritual over the course of 1 hour, which can be done during a short rest. At the conclusion of the ritual, your spectral companion gains one of the following benefits of your choice:

Enlarge. Your spectral companion can use a bonus action on its turn to double its size in all dimensions. This growth increases its size by one category—from Medium to Large. While enlarged, your companion's melee attacks deal an extra 1d6 radiant or necrotic damage (your choice). Your spectral companion can return to normal size on its turn using a bonus action.

Enfeeble. As an action, your spectral companion can make a special attack that saps the strength from an enemy within 60 feet of it. The companion makes a ranged spell attack. On a hit, the target deals only half damage with weapon attacks that use Strength until the end of its next turn.

Entangle. As an action, your companion can attempt to restrain a target with spectral tendrils. The target must succeed on a Strength saving throw against your spell save DC. On a failed save, the target is restrained. The target can repeat the saving throw at the end of each of its turns, ending the effect on itself on a success.

CLAIM THE WICKED

At 18th level, you can use an action to create a portal that summons a creature for judgment. You speak the name of a specific creature (a pseudonym, title, or nickname doesn't work) and create a portal within 60 feet of you.

Another portal opens in the named creature's immediate vicinity and draws the creature through it to the nearest unoccupied space on your side of the portal. The portal vanishes instantly after the summoned creature appears.

The creature must then succeed on a Wisdom saving throw or become frightened of you for 1 minute. The creature can repeat the saving throw at the end of each of its turns, ending the effect on itself on a success.

This feature can summon a creature on the same plane of existence as you, or a creature on a different plane. Deities and other planar rulers can prevent portals created by this feature from opening in their presence or anywhere within their domains.

Once you use this feature, you cannot use it again until you finish a long rest.

Felblade Spell List

1st Level
Bane
Charm Person
Command
Compelled Duel
Detect Evil and Good
Detect Magic
Dissonant Wispers
Hellish Rebuke
Hex
Identify
Inflict Wounds
Protection from Evil and Good
Ray of Sickness

2nd Level
Blindness/Deafness
Crown of Madness
Detect Thoughts
Gentle Repose
Heat Metal
Hold Person
Ray of Enfeeblement
See Invisibility
Silence
Web
Zone of Truth

3rd Level
Bestow Curse
Dispel Magic
Fear
Remove Curse
Slow
Speak with Dead
Vampiric Touch

4th Level
Blight
Dominate Beast
Confusion
Locate Creature
Phantasmal Killer

5th Level
Contagion
Dominate Person
Hold Monster
Planar Binding

CHAPTER 4: FERROCLAD

A bugbear chieftain raises a greatclub to crush a cowering villager. Before the club lands, a metal form descends from the sky and sends the chieftain flying with a single blow from its huge fist. The faceplate in the figure's helm retracts, revealing the smiling face of a half-orc.

Extending his metal-clad hand, a young male elf bombards a goblin encampment with a fiery explosion. A voice from the elf's armor warns him of an approaching goblin raiding party, giving him just enough time to escape.

Inventors and metalworkers, ferroclads wear the signature products of their research: mechanized suits of magical armor. Ferroclads admire the works of artificers, but favor designs that empower them to both withstand and execute formidable attacks in combat.

BRILLIANT DESIGNERS

Crafting and invention define a ferroclad, and each ferroclad's armor represents the apex of their research and experimentation.

Anyone with the proper training and physique can wear plate armor. A ferroclad's armor only functions as a result of their knowledge of magic and engineering, and thanks to their complete understanding of the armor's mechanisms.

Most Ferroclads approach their armor with a bold pragmatism. A typical armor suit will include interchangeable components in order to facilitate upgrade, repair, and to enable the installation of specialized parts called modules. Modules provide support functions and make the armor more versatile without compromising its basic design.

Ferroclad armors take many forms. However, most ferroclads specialize either in armors built for melee combat, or armors that perform best at long range.

EXPLORERS AND SCHOLARS

Ferroclads share a passion for creating the perfect armor, but learn their skills from diverse sources. Some ferroclads study under the tutelage of a master ferroclad or

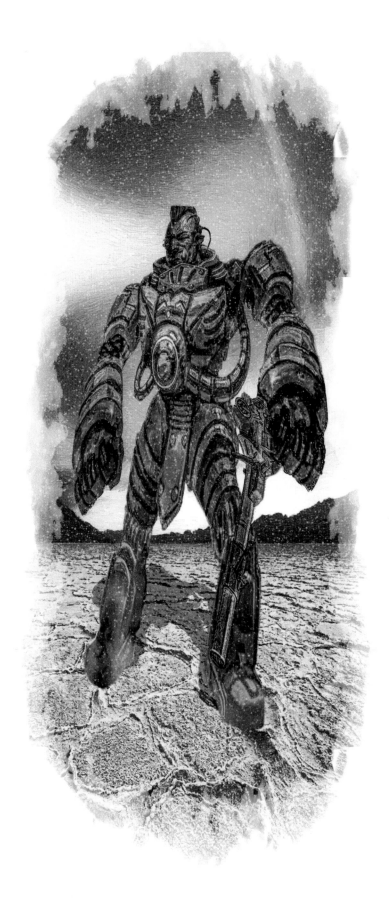

artificer, leaving after they craft their first working armor design. A ferroclad could begin as a novice mage, a blacksmith's apprentice, or an artisan.

Ferroclads gravitate towards adventuring careers to uncover magic items, lost armor schematics left by master ferroclads, and rare materials to incorporate into experimental designs.

The Ferroclad – Class Table

Level	Proficiency Bonus	Features
1st	+2	Ferroclad Armor, Ferroclad Specialist
2nd	+2	Armor Modules (1)
3rd	+2	Ferroclad Specialist Feature
4th	+2	Ability Score Improvement
5th	+3	Extra Attack
6th	+3	Armor Modules (2), Armor Reinforcement (+1)
7th	+3	Ferroclad Specialist Feature
8th	+3	Ability Score Improvement
9th	+4	Ferroclad Specialist Feature
10th	+4	Sentient Armor
11th	+4	Armor Modules (3)
12th	+4	Ability Score Improvement, Armor Reinforcement (+2)
13th	+5	Ferroclad Specialist Feature
14th	+5	Construct Command
15th	+5	Armor Modules (4)
16th	+5	Ability Score Improvement
17th	+6	Ferroclad Specialist Feature
18th	+6	Armor Reinforcement (+3)
19th	+6	Ability Score Improvement
20th	+6	Master Armorer

CREATING A FERROCLAD

When creating your ferroclad character, think about your character's early work and training. Did you learn with the guidance of a mentor, or experiment on your own? If you have a mentor, what is your current relationship with them? Do you seek your mentor out for advice, view them as a rival, or believe that you have surpassed them?

Next, think about your vision for the perfect armor. How close have you come to realizing your vision? What would bring you closer to perfecting your design? How far will you go to make new discoveries?

Ferroclads frequently encounter other ferroclads and artificers in their travels. These meetings might lead to friendly collaboration among good-aligned explorers, or stir up intense—even violent—competition between evil-aligned individuals.

Armor Materials

While the term "ferroclad" is derived from an ancient word for iron, most designs consist of several materials including iron, copper, steel, leather, and small amounts of precious metals or gems. Ferroclads typically paint their armor with bold colors in order to draw attention to their handiwork.

QUICK BUILD

You can make a ferroclad quickly by following these suggestions. First, make Intelligence your highest ability score, followed by Constitution. Second, choose the guild artisan or sage background.

CLASS FEATURES

As a ferroclad, you gain the following class features.

HIT POINTS

Hit Dice: 1d10 per ferroclad level
Hit Points at 1st Level: 10 + your Constitution modifier
Hit Points at Higher Levels: 1d10 (or 6) + your Constitution modifier per ferroclad level after 1st

PROFICIENCIES

Armor: All armor, shields
Weapons: Simple weapons

Tools: Smith's tools, and one from Alchemists's supplies, Cobbler's tools, Leatherworker's tools, and Tinker's tools

Saving Throws: Strength, Intelligence
Skills: Choose three from Arcana, Athletics, History, Investigation, Medicine, Nature, Persuasion, and Sleight of Hand

EQUIPMENT

You start with the following equipment, in addition to the equipment granted by your background:

- leather armor
- (a) any two simple weapons, or (b) any martial weapon (if proficient)
- (a) a light crossbow and 20 bolts or (b) any simple weapon
- Smith's tools and one other set of artisan's tools with which you are proficient
- (a) a dungeoneer's pack or (b) a scholar's pack

FERROCLAD ARMOR

At 1st level, you craft a suit of mechanical plate armor using a combination of arcane magic and your knowledge of engineering and metallurgy. This armor is called Ferroclad Armor.

The armor is a suit of magical plate armor with a base AC of 18. You learn to reinforce the armor for added protection as you develop new armor designs. Your improvements yield a bonus to AC when you reach certain levels in this class: 6th level (+1), 12th level (+2), and 18th level (+3).

Your Ferroclad Armor showcases your finest work and only operates at peak performance when worn by you. The armor allows for free use of your hands, including all weapon proficiencies, skill proficiencies, tool proficiencies, and somatic spell components.

You gain the following benefits while wearing your Ferroclad Armor:

- You have a flying speed of 30 feet, and your jump distance is doubled
- You have advantage on Strength checks and Strength saving throws
- You can use Intelligence instead of Strength or Dexterity for your weapon attack and

damage rolls, and for your ferroclad class features and abilities.

- Your speed is not reduced by the armor, even if you do not meet the Strength ability score requirement for other suits of plate armor.

If you lose your Ferroclad Armor, you can create a new suit over the course of five days of work (eight hours each day) by expending 200 gp worth of metal and other raw materials.

As an object, the armor's master crafting and magical nature render it nigh-indestructible. The armor is immune to all damage short of attacks made by a deity. At your Game Master's discretion, extraordinary damage, such as submerging the armor in lava for hours, might also destroy it. Your body suffers damage and other harmful effects as normal while wearing the armor.

Some of your ferroclad features require your target to make a saving throw to resist the feature's effects. The saving throw DC is calculated as follows:

Ferroclad save DC
= 8 + your proficiency bonus + your Intelligence modifier

IMPROVED MENDING

Beginning at 1st level, you learn the *mending* cantrip. You don't need to provide the material component when casting *mending* with this feature.

When you cast *mending* on an item you create, such as your Ferroclad Armor or modules, the spell restores the item's magical properties (if any) and function in addition to repairing any physical damage to the item, provided that the damage is no larger than 1 foot in any dimension.

FERROCLAD SPECIALIST

Also at 1st level, you choose the type of Ferroclad Specialist you are: Pulverizer or Destroyer, both of which are detailed at the end of the class description. Your choice grants you features at 1st level and again at 3rd, 7th, 9th, 13th, and 17th level.

ARMOR MODULES

Starting at 2nd level, you can modify your Ferroclad Armor with devices that grant additional abilities.

You can install one Armor Module at 2nd level, choosing from the modules at the end of the class description. You can equip more armor modules when you reach certain levels in this class: 6th level (2), 12th level (3), and 15th level (4).

You can replace an Armor Module with a different one over the course of 1 hour of work, which can be done during a short rest.

ABILITY SCORE IMPROVEMENT

When you reach 4th level, and again at 8th, 12th, 16th, and 19th level, you can increase one ability score of your choice by 2, or you can increase two ability scores of your choice by 1.

If you are using options from *5e Legendary Heroes* to create a heroic character, you can increase an ability score up to a maximum of 30. Otherwise, you can't increase an ability score above 20 using this feature.

EXTRA ATTACK

Beginning at 5th level, you can attack twice, instead of once, whenever you take the Attack action on your turn.

SENTIENT ARMOR

By 10th level, you have made a discovery that allows you to imbue your Ferroclad Armor with self-awareness and personality.

You can activate the armor's sentience over the course of 8 hours of work, which can be completed during a long rest. The armor's personality then functions as a character under the Game Master's control.

The sentient armor has the following additional properties:

- The armor shares your alignment, with an Intelligence of 14, a Wisdom of 10, and a Charisma of 8. It has hearing and darkvision out to a range of 120 feet. While wearing the armor, you have darkvision out to a range of 120 feet.
- The armor can speak, read, and understand every language you know, and can communicate with you telepathically out to a range of 500 feet.

While wearing your Ferroclad Armor, you gain one of the following features of your choice.

Recall. You gain proficiency in the History, Nature, and Religion skills. If you're already proficient in any of those skills, your proficiency bonus is doubled for any check you make with them.

Threat Detection. You have advantage on initiative rolls. If you are surprised at the beginning of combat and aren't incapacitated, you can act normally on your first turn.

Telescopic Vision. You can see up to 1 mile away with no difficulty, able to discern even fine details as though looking at something no more than 100 feet away from you. In addition, dim light doesn't impose disadvantage on your Wisdom (Perception) checks.

CONSTRUCT COMMAND

Beginning at 14th level, your knowledge of engineering and arcane magic has advanced so much that you can take command of artificial creatures.

As an action, you can attempt to control a construct within 60 feet. It must succeed on a Wisdom saving throw or be charmed by you for 1 hour. If you or creatures that are friendly to you are fighting the construct, it has advantage on the saving throw.

While the construct is charmed, you can use a bonus action to mentally command it if the construct is within 60 feet of you.

You decide what action the construct will take, and where it moves during its next turn. Alternatively, you can issue a general command, such as to protect your comrades or attack anyone who comes within its reach. If you issue no commands, the construct will defend you and itself against hostile creatures.

The creature is under your control for 1 hour, after which it stops obeying any command you've given it. Once you successfully take control of a construct, you cannot use this feature again until you finish a short or long rest.

MASTER ARMORER

Starting at 20th level, you make a breakthrough that stands as your greatest achievement in armor design. While wearing your Ferroclad Armor, you gain one of the following features of your choice.

Assimilation. You develop a process to meld certain magic items into your armor over the course of 1 hour of work. Instead of attuning to a magic item, you can make a DC 15 Intelligence check using your Smith's tools. On a failed Intelligence check, the item proves incompatible with your Ferroclad Armor and cannot be assimilated. You can still attune to the item and wield it as normal, provided that you meet the item's attunement prerequisites.

On a success, you integrate the item into your Ferroclad Armor. You gain any benefits (except bonuses to AC) derived from attuning to and/or wielding the item. However, assimilating the item does not count towards the maximum number of magic items you can be attuned to at a time. This process does not permanently alter or damage the item.

You can assimilate up to two magic items using this feature, performing the process over the course of 1 hour of work each time. You make another DC 15 Intelligence check to replace an assimilated item with a different one over the course of 1 hour of work, by expending 50 gp worth of metal and other raw materials.

Your Game Master has the final say on whether you can assimilate a particular magic item. Attempting to merge your Ferroclad Armor with a piece of magic armor, a shield, or a magic weapon confers no benefit, and automatically fails.

Automation. You improve your Ferroclad Armor's sentience to allow for remote control. When you are not wearing your armor but are within range of the telepathic link with your Ferroclad Armor (500 feet), you can use a bonus action on each of your turns to mentally command it. The armor rolls its own initiative and takes its own turn in the turn order.

You decide what action the armor will take, and where it moves on its turn. Alternatively, you can issue a general command, such as to protect your comrades or attack anyone who comes within its reach. If you issue no commands, the armor will defend you and itself against hostile creatures.

Your armor can use all of its attached components, weapons, and modules while controlled, with a Strength of 16, a Dexterity of 10, and a Constitution of 18. The armor uses your proficiency bonus, and is proficient with all saving throws.

If you are reduced to 0 hit points, the armor will take the Dash action and use its movement to move to the nearest unoccupied space next to you via the shortest possible route. When the armor reaches you, it will use its Action and movement on each of its turns to defend you from further harm to the best of its ability.

FERROCLAD SPECIALIST

Ferroclads create armors with many different forms. Most ferroclads focus on designs that emphasize overwhelming attacks in melee combat, or on devastating long-range attacks.

PULVERIZER

Pulverizers specialize in armor designed to deliver overpowering blows with melee weapons and unarmed strikes. Iconic Pulverizer armors incorporate reinforced gauntlets, net launchers, and oversized melee weapons.

BONUS PROFICIENCIES

When you choose this specialization at first level, you gain proficiency with martial weapons.

ROCK CRUSHER

Also starting when you choose this specialization at 1st level, you can roll a d4 in place of the normal damage of your unarmed strikes. This die changes when you reach certain levels in this class: 5th level (d6), 11th level (d8), 17th level (d10), and 20th level (d12).

Additionally, your unarmed strikes deal double damage to objects and structures.

ROCKET GAUNTLETS

At 3rd level, you modify your gauntlets to launch them at enemies.

You gain a ranged weapon attack that you can use with the Attack action. The attack has a normal range of 30 feet, and a maximum range of 60 feet. You are proficient with it, and you add your Intelligence modifier to its attack and damage rolls. Its

damage is bludgeoning, and its damage die is a d4.

This die changes when you reach certain levels in this class: 5th level (d6), 11th level (d8), 17th level (d10), and 20th level (d12).

You have enough control over the gauntlet's flight path to steer around obstacles, ignoring half cover and three-quarters cover. The gauntlet returns to your hand immediately after the attack, even if the attack misses.

IRON DEFENSE

At 7th level, you gain one of the following features of your choice.

Net Cannon. You modify your armor to fire a net attached to a metal cable or chain. The net is a martial ranged weapon with a normal range of 10 feet, and a maximum range of 20 feet.

On a hit, a Large or smaller creature is restrained until it is freed. The net has no effect on creatures that are formless, or creatures that are Huge or larger. A creature can use its action to a make a DC 12 Strength check, freeing itself on a success. Dealing 10 slashing damage to the net (AC 13) also frees the creature without harming it, ending the effect and destroying the net. Your improved *mending* cantrip will fully repair the net.

You can use a bonus action on your turn to recall the net, immediately freeing any creature restrained by it.

Iron Hail. You equip your armor with a device that sprays ball bearings and sharp bits of scrap metal.

When you are hit with a melee attack, you can use your reaction to activate the device. The attacker must make a Dexterity saving throw, taking 4d6 piercing damage on a failed save, or half as much damage on a successful one.

Once you use this feature, you must finish a short or long rest before you can use it again.

IRON ASSAULT

At 9th level, you gain one of the following features of your choice.

Iron Sting. You install retractable metal spikes into your gauntlets. When you hit a creature with an unarmed strike or Rocket

Gauntlet, the target takes an additional 1d6 piercing damage.

Oversized Weapon. Choose any nonmagical melee weapon with which you are proficient. You forge an oversized copy of that weapon, which you can wield with the augmented strength of your Ferroclad Armor. On a hit, the weapon deals an additional 1d6 bludgeoning damage.

The weapon gains the Heavy property in addition to its normal properties. If the weapon already has the Heavy property, Medium or smaller creatures not wearing Ferroclad Armor have disadvantage on attack rolls made with the weapon.

Extra Attack

Starting at 13th level, you can attack three times whenever you take the Attack action on your turn.

Giant Breaker

By 17th level, your research and field tests allow you to make major improvements to your Ferroclad Armor.

You can use an action on your turn to grow in size, increasing your size category by two sizes—from Medium to Huge, for example. If there isn't enough room to increase your size to Huge, you attain the maximum possible size in the space available. You can use a bonus action on your turn to end this effect and return to your previous size.

Your Ferroclad Armor and weapons grow to match your new size. While enlarged, your weapon attacks and unarmed strikes deal 2d6 extra damage.

Destroyer

Destroyers engineer armor designs that project high-powered energy blasts, often taking advantage of their flight capabilities to keep enemies at long range.

Charge Cannon

Beginning when you choose this specialization at 1st level, you create a ranged weapon called a Charge Cannon. The Charge Cannon could take the form of a shoulder- or wrist-mounted tube, a handheld firearm, or apertures in the palms of your Ferroclad Armor's gauntlets.

You are proficient with the Charge Cannon. The cannon is a two-handed ranged weapon that deals 2d6 force damage. Its normal range is 150 feet, and its maximum range is 500 feet.

When you use your Action to make a ranged weapon attack with your Charge Cannon, you can use a bonus action to accumulate energy in the weapon until the end of your next turn. If you do, your next ranged weapon attack with your Charge Cannon deals an additional 1d6 force damage.

You lose the charge if you take any damage, or if you attack with a weapon other than your Charge Cannon.

Mega Charge

At 3rd level, you improve your Charge Cannon design to contain more arcane energy. If you use a bonus action on two or more consecutive turns to collect energy in your Charge Cannon, you can make a special explosive attack with your Charge Cannon. For 1 minute, your next Charge Cannon attack causes an explosion of arcane energy in a 10-foot radius sphere at a point within 150 feet.

Each creature in that area must make a Dexterity saving throw, taking 4d6 force damage on a failed save, or half as much damage on a successful save.

Improved Flight

At 7th level, you gain one of the following features of your choice.

Evasive Dash. You can take the Dash action as a bonus action on each of your turns. In addition, when a hostile creature moves within 5 feet of you, you can use your reaction to move up to half your speed. This movement does not provoke opportunity attacks.

Swift Flight. You gain a flying speed of 60 feet, and your jump distance is tripled.

Elemental Shots

Beginning at 9th level when you make a ranged weapon attack using your Charge Cannon, you can choose to deal acid, cold, fire, or lightning damage instead of force damage. You can choose the damage type before or after making an attack roll, but before any effects of the attack are applied.

In addition, you gain one of the following features of your choice.

Overwatch. When a hostile creature moves within 15 feet of you, you can use you reaction to fire a shot. On a hit, the target takes 2d6 force damage, and must make a Strength saving throw. On a failed save, the creature is knocked prone by the impact.

Target Finder. As a bonus action on each of your turns, you can take aim at a creature within your Charge Cannon's range, provided that the creature is at least 30 feet away from you. You may add +3 to any ranged weapon attack rolls against the target.

In addition, attacking the target within your Charge Cannon's long range doesn't impose disadvantage on your ranged weapon attack rolls. The effect ends if you make an attack against a different creature, or if you make an attack with a spell, effect, or weapon other than your Charge Cannon.

RAPID FIRE

By 13th level, your Charge Cannon can fire shots in quick succession at the cost of accuracy.

When you use the Attack action on your turn to make ranged weapon attacks using your Charge Cannon and no other weapons, you can use a bonus action to make up to four additional ranged weapon attacks using your Charge Cannon. Each additional attack suffers a cumulative -3 penalty to the attack roll.

Once you use this feature to make additional attacks, you cannot use it again for 1 minute.

ARCANE ARTILLERY

Starting at 17th level, you perfect your Ferroclad Armor's ability to annihilate foes at range, by releasing all of your armor's accumulated arcane energy in a 40-foot radius sphere centered on a point within 300 feet.

Each creature in the area must make a Dexterity saving throw. A creature takes 40d6 force damage on a failed save, or half as much damage on a successful one. If a creature fails the save by 5 or more, it also

takes 6d6 bludgeoning damage and is knocked prone.

If this damage reduces a creature to 0 hit points, it is vaporized. Once you use this feature, you cannot use it again until you finish a long rest.

ARMOR MODULES

Starting at 2nd level, you can choose from among the following Armor Module options. You must be wearing your Ferroclad Armor to gain the benefit of any modules.

With your Game Master's approval, you can create additional Armor Module options of your own. Your Game Master has the final say on any new Armor Module.

AQUATIC EXPLORATOR

You gain a swim speed of 30 feet and can breathe underwater.

ARCANE BURST

When a creature hits you with a melee attack, you can use your reaction to release a wave of force in a 15-foot cone. Creatures in the area must make a Strength saving throw. On a failed saving throw, a creature takes 1d6 force damage and is pushed 10 feet away from you.

AUGMENTED SENSORS

You have blindsight within a 20-foot radius. In addition, you can see through objects that are up to 1 foot thick within 20 feet of you.

CHILLING RAY

You gain a ranged spell attack that you can use once on each of your turns with the Attack action. The attack has a range of 30 feet. You are proficient with it, and you add your Intelligence modifier to its attack and damage rolls. On a hit, the attack deals 2d6 cold damage, and the target's speed is reduced by 10 feet until the start of your next turn.

CORROSIVE RAY

You gain a ranged spell attack that you can use once on each of your turns with the Attack action. The attack has a range of 30 feet. You are proficient with it, and you add your Intelligence modifier to its attack and damage rolls. On a hit, the attack deals 2d6 acid damage.

If the target is wearing nonmagical armor, it also suffers a cumulative -1 penalty to AC. If its penalty drops to -5, the target's armor is destroyed. If the target is wielding a shield, the shield is destroyed if the penalty drops to -2.

FLASH PROJECTOR

As an action, you can emit a momentary flare of blinding light in a 30-foot radius sphere centered on your Ferroclad Armor. The sphere is bright light and sheds dim light for an additional 60 feet.

Each creature that can see you within the area of bright light must make a Constitution saving throw. On a failed save, a creature is blinded for 1 minute. A creature blinded by this module makes another Constitution saving throw at the end of each of its turns. On a successful save, it is no longer blinded.

MAGNETIC NEEDLER

You outfit your Ferroclad Armor with a weapon that fires poisoned steel needles, called a Magnetic Needler.

You are proficient with the Magnetic Needler. The weapon is a one-handed ranged weapon that deals 1d4 piercing damage. Its normal range is 80 feet, and its maximum range is 320 feet.

On a hit, a creature must make a DC 15 Constitution saving throw, taking 3d6 poison damage on a failed save, or half as much damage on a successful one.

OVERDRIVE

As an action, you can override your Ferroclad Armor's safety mechanisms. For 1 minute, your speed is doubled, you gain a +2 bonus to AC, you have advantage on Dexterity saving throws, and you gain an additional action on each of your turns. That action can be used only to take the Attack (one weapon attack only), Dash, Disengage, Hide, or Use an Object actions. When the effect ends, you can't move or take actions until after your next turn.

Once you use this feature, you must finish a short or long rest before you can use it again.

PSYCHIC SHIELD

You gain resistance to psychic damage. In addition, you have advantage on saving throws against being charmed, frightened, and stunned.

SHOCK ARMOR

When a creature hits you with a melee attack, you can use your reaction to deal 1d6 lightning damage to the attacker. The target can't take reactions until the start of its next turn.

SMOKE LAUNCHER

You can use an action to expel a 20-foot radius sphere of thick gray smoke from your Ferroclad Armor. The sphere spreads around corners, and its area is heavily obscured. The smoke lasts for 1 minute or until a wind of moderate or greater speed (at least 10 miles per hour) disperses it.

STEALTH FIELD

Your Ferroclad Armor does not impose disadvantage on Dexterity (Stealth) checks. In addition, you have advantage on Dexterity (Stealth) checks while in areas of dim light and darkness.

GM Tip: Item Dependent Classes

Not all classes function equally well in every campaign, but certain classes warrant special consideration. Item-dependent character classes, like the ferroclad and artificer, rely on their crafted items in order to use most of their class features and abilities. Deprived of these items, the character becomes much less effective in combat.

When planning and running your campaign, think about whether you will include scenarios in which the characters will not have access to their equipment (e.g., imprisonment, covert operations, item seizure). If the campaign will feature these scenarios on a regular basis, then warn players against choosing an item-dependent class.

If an item-dependent character loses their items, you might help them in the following ways:

- Give the party a chance to spend time in a laboratory or workshop where the item-dependent character can craft replacement items, possibly without expending gp.
- Let the character retrieve their items

- Allow the character to use a functionally-identical item, perhaps made by a colleague or rival, until they can craft their own.
- Have a friendly NPC smuggle the item(s)

VARIANT: CRAFTING MORE ARMORS

At your Game Master's discretion, you can craft simplified Ferroclad Armor suits and teach others to use them. Starting at 3rd level, you can craft a less sophisticated copy of your Ferroclad Armor over the course of five days of work (eight hours each day) by expending 150 gp worth of metal and other raw materials.

This armor is a suit of magical splint armor with a +1 bonus to AC. While wearing the armor, you and creatures proficient with it gain the following benefits:

- You can use a bonus action to activate the armor's flight capabilities. If you do, you gain a flying speed of 20 feet until the end of your next turn. Once used, this property of the armor can't be used again for 1 minute.
- You have a +1 bonus to Strength checks and Strength saving throws.
- You gain a ranged spell attack that you can use once on each of your turns with the Attack action. The attack has a range of 30 feet. You are proficient with it, and you add your Intelligence modifier to its attack and damage rolls. On a hit, the attack deals 1d6 force damage. If you chose the Destroyer specialization, the attack's damage die changes from a d6 to a d8.
- If you chose the Pulverizer specialization, your unarmed strike uses a d4 for damage.

WEARING FERROCLAD ARMOR

You are proficient with the armor you craft. However, creatures other than you, including creatures with proficiency in heavy armor, require special training in order to gain proficiency with your simplified Ferroclad Armor. Creatures wearing armor who lack proficiency with it have disadvantage on all ability checks, savings throws, or attack rolls that involve Strength or Dexterity, and can't cast spells.

You can train others to operate the simplified armor over the course of 30 days. You can train a number of creatures equal to your Intelligence modifier at any time, provided that each creature has access to their own suit of Ferroclad Armor. After a creature spends the requisite amount of time training, they become proficient with the simplified Ferroclad Armor. You can choose how much to charge (if anything) for such training.

CHAPTER 5: PROTEAN

A blue dragonborn transforms into a gigantic cave bear as he sprints toward a dark elf patrol. Two more bears appear from the darkness, cutting off the elves' escape route. Without a sound, the bears advance on the elves in a perfectly coordinated assault.

Two humanoid wolf-like creatures grapple in the center of a moonlit forest clearing. One creature has glowing red eyes and bared fangs. The other figure focuses with almost-human eyes, and wields claws that glow in the darkness.

A glancing claw swipe from the glowing-handed wolf transforms the red-eyed creature into a shocked young half-elf. As the half-elf changes, the glowing-handed wolf relaxes, reverting to her human form.

More mercurial than druids and less bestial than true lycanthropes, proteans practice a unique form of shapechanging.

ADAPT AND PREVAIL

Proteans draw their power from nature; specifically, the vibrant and ever-changing energies that animate all living things. Many proteans worship deities of life, fertility, or nature.

Shapechanging defines proteans. Proteans can transform into beast forms, fearsome hybrid forms, and into almost any humanoid race. A few powerful proteans can morph into monstrosities, elementals, or dragons.

FIERCE PROTECTORS

Like druids, proteans commune in small groups called Circles. Circles hunt creatures that have no rightful place in nature, such as aberrations, fiends, and undead.

If a protean Circle encounters evil lycanthropes, they will first seek to cure victims of the curse of lycanthropy. If any lycanthropes embrace their curse and continue to prey upon innocent creatures, then the proteans will destroy the incorrigible lycanthropes.

Proteans often work together with druids and rangers to combat threats to the natural order. Most proteans will also join with other adventurers to protect civilized regions, and to hunt dangerous foes. As long as a protean can calm potential allies who mistake them for lycanthropes, proteans make ideal adventuring companions.

The Protean – Class Table

Level	Proficiency Bonus	Features
1st	+2	Protean Circle, Form Shift
2nd	+2	Form Mastery
3rd	+2	Protean Circle Feature
4th	+2	Ability Score Improvement
5th	+3	Extra Attack
6th	+3	Protean Circle Feature, Wild Strike
7th	+3	Rejuvenating Transformation
8th	+3	Ability Score Improvement
9th	+4	Protean Circle Feature
10th	+4	Adaptive Form
11th	+4	Binding Strike
12th	+4	Ability Score Improvement
13th	+5	Frenzy
14th	+5	Protean Circle Feature
15th	+5	Resilient Form
16th	+5	Ability Score Improvement
17th	+6	Rebirth
18th	+6	Protean Circle Feature
19th	+6	Ability Score Improvement
20th	+6	Mythic Transformation

CREATING A PROTEAN

As you create your protean character, first consider why your character chose to learn the secrets of shapeshifting. Did a loved one succumb to the curse of lycanthropy, or die in a lycanthrope's murderous rampage? Were you saved from the curse of lycanthropy by a benevolent protean who served as your mentor?

Second, think about how your character views shapechanging. Many good-aligned proteans view shapeshifting to impersonate other sentient creatures as an evil act. Evil proteans will not hesitate to murder (and assume the identities of) their victims for personal gain.

QUICK BUILD

You can make a protean quickly by following these suggestions. First, Charisma should be your highest ability score, followed by Constitution. Second, choose the hermit or outlander background.

CLASS FEATURES

As a protean, you gain the following class features.

HIT POINTS

Hit Dice: 1d12 per protean level
Hit Points at 1st Level: 12 + your Constitution modifier
Hit Points at Higher Levels: 1d12 (or 7) + your Constitution modifier per protean level after 1st

PROFICIENCIES

Armor: light armor, medium armor, shields
Weapons: Simple weapons
Tools: None

Saving Throws: Constitution, Charisma
Skills: Choose two from Arcana, Animal Handling, Deception, History, Medicine, Nature, Perception, Religion, and Survival

EQUIPMENT

You start with the following equipment, in addition to the equipment granted by your background:

• leather armor

• any two simple weapons
• (*a*) a light crossbow and 20 bolts or (*b*) five javelins
• (*a*) a dungeoneer's pack or (*b*) an explorer's pack

FORM SHIFT

Starting at 1st level, you can use a bonus action to transform into a beast or beast-humanoid hybrid shape, choosing a beast that you have seen before.

You can revert to your humanoid form by using a bonus action on your turn. You automatically revert if you fall unconscious, drop to 0 hit points, or die.

You can assume the shape of a beast that has a challenge rating as high as your protean level. For example, at 5th level you could transform into a beast with a challenge rating of 5 or lower.

Many beasts have natural weapons in the form of claws, horns, talons, or stingers. You are proficient with your form's natural weapons. You can use Charisma, instead of Strength or Dexterity, for the attack and damage rolls of your natural melee and ranged weapons.

The Natural Weapons table provides damage values for the most common natural weapons. You can use the damage values detailed in a beast's game statistics, or consult the Natural Weapons table to determine the damage of your natural weapon attacks.

Natural Weapons

Name	Damage
Beak	1d6 piercing
Bite	1d8 piercing
Claw	1d6 slashing
Gore	1d8 piercing
Hooves	1d8 bludgeoning
Ram	2d6 bludgeoning
Sting	1d10 piercing
Tail	2d6 bludgeoning
Tusk	1d12 slashing

BEAST FORM

While you are transformed into a beast, the following rules apply:

- Your game statistics are replaced by the statistics of the beast, but you retain your alignment, personality, and Intelligence, Wisdom, and Charisma scores. You retain all of your skill and saving throw proficiencies, but do not gain those of the creature.
- You can use the actions available to the creature, such as attacks or special abilities. If the creature has any legendary or lair actions, you can't use them.
- When you transform, you assume the beast's hit points and Hit Dice. When you revert to your normal form, you return to the number of hit points you had before you transformed. However, if you revert as a result of dropping to 0 hit points, any excess damage carries over to your normal form.
- You can't cast spells, and your ability to speak or take any action that requires hands is limited to the capabilities of your beast form. Transforming doesn't break your concentration on a spell you've already cast, however, or prevent you from taking actions that are part of a spell, such as *flaming sphere*, that you've already cast.
- You retain the benefit of any features from your class, race, or other source and can use them if the beast form is physically capable of doing so. Provided that the beast form has the requisite sense organs (e.g., eyes, nose, ears) you also retain the use of any special senses, such as darkvision, even if the beast does not normally possess those special senses.
- You choose whether your equipment falls to the ground in your space, merges with your new form, or is worn by it. Worn equipment functions as normal, but your Game Master decides whether it is practical for the new form to wear a piece of equipment, based on the creature's size and shape. Worn equipment doesn't change size or shape to match the new form, and any equipment that the new form can't wear must either fall to the ground or merge with it. You retain the benefits of any worn or merged magic items.

Hybrid Form

The same rules used for your beast form apply while you are transformed into a beast-humanoid hybrid, with the following differences:

- You can cast spells, speak, and take actions that require hands. If your hybrid form has claws or talons, then your GM might decide to impose a minor penalty on skill checks that depend on careful use of your hands.
- You can use the beast's natural weapons in addition to melee and ranged weapons.

Some of your protean features require your target to make a saving throw to resist the feature's effects. The saving throw DC is calculated as follows:

Protean save DC
= 8 + your proficiency bonus
+ your Charisma modifier

Protean Circle

By 1st level, you have chosen to identify with a circle of proteans: the Circle of the Pack, or the Circle of Metamorphosis, both detailed at the end of the class description. Your choice grants you features at 1st level and again at 3rd, 6th, 9th, 14th, and 18th level.

Form Mastery

Beginning at 2nd level, you know the *disguise self* spell, and you can cast it at will.

The nature magic flowing through you makes you immune to the curse of lycanthropy. If you are afflicted by the curse of lycanthropy when you reach 2nd level, the curse immediately ends. In addition, your form can't be altered by magic or other means, unless you allow it.

Ability Score Improvement

When you reach 4th level, and again at 8th, 12th, 16th, and 19th level, you can increase one ability score of your choice by 2, or you can increase two ability scores of your choice by 1.

If you are using options from *5e Legendary Heroes* to create a heroic character, you can increase an ability score up to a maximum of 30. Otherwise, you can't increase an ability score above 20 using this feature.

Extra Attack

Beginning at 5th level, you can attack twice, instead of once, whenever you take the Attack action on your turn.

Wild Strike

Starting at 6th level, your natural weapon attacks count as magical for the purpose of overcoming resistance and immunity to nonmagical attacks and damage.

Rejuvenating Transformation

By 7th level, the magic that empowers your shapechanging can heal your wounds. When you use Form Shift to revert to your normal form, you can regain hit points equal to half of your hit point maximum.

Once you use this feature, you must finish a short or long rest before you can use it again.

Adaptive Form

At 10th level, you learn to alter your form to withstand damage and harmful effects. On your turn, you can use a bonus action to gain resistance to acid, cold, fire, force, lightning, necrotic, poison, psychic, radiant, or thunder damage (your choice) for 1 minute.

Alternatively, you can use a bonus action to end one spell affecting you.

You can use this feature a number of times equal to your Charisma modifier (a minimum of once). You regain expended uses when you finish a long rest.

Binding Strike

Starting at 11th level, your natural weapon attacks disrupt the forms of lycanthropes and other shapeshifters.

When you hit a creature with your natural weapons that is not in its original form, the creature must make a Charisma saving throw. On a failed save, the creature reverts to its original form and can't assume a different form for 1 minute.

You know whether a creature is forced to make the saving throw, and whether a creature succeeds or fails on its saving throw.

Frenzy

Beginning at 13th level, you can use a bonus action on your turn to enter a bestial rage. While raging, you gain the following benefits:

- If you are not already transformed, you immediately assume a beast or beast-humanoid hybrid form.
- You roll an additional damage die when determining the damage of your natural weapon attacks.
- You can attack three times whenever you take the Attack action on your turn.

Your rage lasts for 1 minute. It ends early if you are knocked unconscious. You can also end your rage on your turn as a bonus action. When your rage ends, you revert to your humanoid form and cannot assume a different shape until the start of your next turn.

Once you use this feature, you cannot use it again until you finish a long rest.

Resilient Form

At 15th level, the life-giving energy of nature makes you immune to disease and poison.

Rebirth

By 17th level, your connection to life energy prevents you from dying. If you die from any cause other than old age, your body reforms in the nearest unoccupied space in 1d4 weeks.

Mythic Transformation

Starting at 20th level, your transformations channel an even greater abundance of life energy. While transformed, you gain the following benefits:

- You regain 1d12 hit points at the start of each of your turns.
- Any severed body members are restored after 2 minutes. If you have the severed part and hold it to the stump, the limb instantaneously knits to the stump.

Protean Circles

Proteans first learn the secrets of shape changing in small groups, called circles. Consisting of only two or three members, protean circles often join forces with local druid circles and rangers who hold similar views on nature.

CIRCLE OF THE PACK

The Circle of the Pack practices transformation as a means to bond with nature, and adopts the protection of living creatures as their common cause. As they learn to draw on more powerful nature magic, these proteans attract a variety of animal companions.

BEAST LORE

When you choose this circle at 1st level, you gain the ability to cast the *beast sense* and *speak with animals* spells, but only as rituals.

PACK LEADER

Also at 1st level, you learn a ritual that creates a powerful bond with a creature of the natural world.

You perform the ritual over the course of 8 hours, which can be done during a long rest. At the conclusion of the ritual, you call forth an animal from the wilderness to serve as a faithful companion.

When you call forth an animal companion, you normally choose a beast that is no larger than Medium and that has a challenge rating of ¼ or lower. However, your Game Master might pick an animal for you, based on the surrounding terrain and on what types of creatures would logically be present in the area.

If your animal companion is ever slain, the magical bond you share allows you to return it to life. With 8 hours of work and the expenditure of 25 gp worth of rare herbs and fine food, you call forth your companion's spirit and use your magic to create a new body for it. You can return an animal companion to life in this manner even if you do not possess any part of its body.

You can perform the ritual again to call forth more animal companions when you reach certain levels in this class: 6th level (2), 9th level (3), 13th level (4), and 20th level (5).

Additionally, when you gain a level in this class, you can choose one of your animal companions and replace it with a different one.

BEAST BOND

Your animal companions obey your commands to the best of their ability. They roll for initiative like other creatures, but you determine their actions, decisions, attitudes, and so on. If you are incapacitated or absent, your companions act on their own.

Your animal companions have abilities and game statistics determined in part by your level. Your companions use your proficiency bonus rather than their own. In addition to the areas where they normally use their proficiency bonus, your animal companions also add their proficiency bonus to their AC and to their damage rolls. Animal companions also become proficient with all saving throws.

For each level you gain after 1st, your animal companions each gain an additional hit die and increase their hit points accordingly.

Whenever you gain the Ability Score Improvement class feature, your companions' abilities also improve. Your companions can each increase one ability score of your choice by 2, or they can increase two ability scores of your choice by 1.

If you are using options from *5e Legendary Heroes* to create a heroic character, you can increase your animal companions' ability scores up to a maximum of 30. Otherwise, you can't increase an ability score above 20 using this feature.

Your companions share your alignment, and their bond is always, "the protean who travels with me is a beloved companion for whom I would gladly give my life."

PACK TACTICS

Beginning at 3rd level, you have advantage on attack rolls against a creature if at least one of your animal companions is within 5 feet of the creature and isn't incapacitated.

LIFESHAPER'S BLESSING

Starting at 6th level, you learn to grant a boon that transforms one of your animal companions.

You perform a ritual over the course of 1 hour to empower one animal companion. The maximum number of animal companions you can call forth decreases by 1, and the empowered companion gains the following benefits:

- Your animal companion can use a bonus action on its turn to double its size in all dimensions for 1 minute. This growth increases its size by one category—normally from Medium to Large. Your companion has advantage on Strength checks and Strength saving throws for the duration, and its natural weapon attacks deal 1d4 extra damage. Once an animal companion increase its size using this feature, it cannot do so again until you finish a short or long rest.
- It gains a +1 bonus to AC.
- Its attacks count as magical for the purposes of overcome resistance and immunity to nonmagical attacks and damage.
- Its movement speed increases by 10 feet.
- It has darkvision out to a range of 60 feet. It is already has darkvision, its range increases by 60 feet

You can grant this boon to one of your animal companions. Your animal companion loses these benefits if you perform the ritual to empower a different animal companion, or if you use an action on your turn to end it.

BEAST TRAINING

By 9th level, you can teach your animal companions to perform more complex actions. You gain one of the following features of your choice.

Protection. If you are the target of a melee attack and one or more of your animal companions is within 5 feet of the attacker, you can use your reaction to command all of your animal companions within range to respond, each using their reaction to make a melee attack against the attacker. If one or more of your animal companions hits the attacker, then the attacker has disadvantage on attack rolls against you until the end of your next turn.

Hamstring. When you or your animal companions hits a creature with a melee attack, the creature's movement speed is halved until the end of your next turn.

Avoidance. Opportunity attacks against you and your animal companions are made with disadvantage.

HEALING BOND

At 14th level, you can channel life energy to sustain yourself and your animal companions. You gain one of the following features of your choice.

Resilience. When you use your Adaptive Form feature to gain resistance to a damage type, you can also confer resistance to that damage type to each of your animal companions within 60 feet of you. If you use your Adaptive Form feature to end a spell that is affecting you, you can also end one spell affecting each of your animal companions within 60 feet of you.

Rejuvenation. When you use your Rejuvenating Transformation feature to regain hit points, each of your animal companions within 60 feet gains temporary hit points equal to twice your protean level.

SUPREME HUNTER

Starting at 18th level, you can use a bonus action on each of your turns to mark a target within 120 feet. You and your animal companions gain the following benefits against marked targets:

- You know the creature's location while it is within 1 mile of you.
- You know if the creature is wounded, and whether it has more than half of its hit points left.
- While within 5 feet of you, the creature provokes opportunity attacks from you and your animal companions even if it takes the Disengage action before leaving your reach.

This effect lasts for 24 hours. The effect immediately ends if you mark a different creature, or if you choose to end if as a bonus action on your turn.

CIRCLE OF METAMORPHOSIS

Proteans adhering to the Circle of Metamorphosis embrace shapeshifting as a reflection of the constant change observed in nature. These proteans seek out and study new creatures, searching for the ideal form for every environment.

MYRIAD FORMS

When you choose this circle at 1st level, select a creature type from among fey, monstrosities, and plants. When you use your Form Shift feature, you can assume the shape of a beast, beast-humanoid hybrid, or any creature of the chosen type that you have seen before with a challenge rating as high as your protean level.

FLUID FORM

Starting at 3rd level, you gain the ability to cast the *alter self* spell as an action. You can use this feature a number of time equal to your Charisma modifier (a minimum of once). You regain all expended uses when you finish a short or long rest.

NATURAL DEFENSE

Beginning at 6th level, you can incorporate a protective modification when you use your Form Shift feature to assume a shape. While transformed, you gain one of the following features of your choice.

Adhesive. As an action, you can spit a 5-foot diameter spray of adhesive at a point within 30 feet. Creatures in the area must succeed on a Dexterity saving throw. On a failed save, the creature is restrained. A creature restrained by the adhesive can use its action to make a Strength check against your shifter save DC. It if succeeds, it is no longer restrained. Once you use this feature, you cannot use it again for 1 minute.

Hardened Carapace. You change your shape to include a shell or chitinous plates. You gain a +1 bonus to AC. In addition, when a creature hits you with a melee attack but does not score a critical hit, the creature cannot attack again until the start of its next turn.

Stunning Screech. As an action, you can emit a piercing screech. Each creature within 20 feet that can hear you must succeed on a Constitution saving throw or be stunned until the end of your next turn. Once you use this feature, you cannot use it again until you finish a short or long rest.

VENOMOUS WEAPONS

By 9th level, you have learned to inject venom with all of your natural weapons. The first time you hit a creature with a melee attack using your natural weapons on your turn, you can force the creature to make a Constitution saving throw against your protean save DC. On a failed save, the creature takes 2d10 poison damage, or half a much on a successful save.

The poison damage increases by 1d10 when you reach certain levels in this class: 13th level (3d10), and 19th level (4d10).

CREATURE ANALYSIS

Starting at 14th level, if you spend at least 1 minute observing or interacting with another creature outside of combat, you learn certain information about its capabilities and characteristics. The GM tells you the up to three of the following facts of your choice:

- Alignment
- Creature type
- One ability score of your choice (you can choose this option multiple times, learning a different ability score each time)
- Damage resistances and immunities (if any)
- Current hit points
- Armor Class
- Saving throw proficiencies (if any)
- Total class levels (if any)
- Legendary and lair actions (if any)

GREATER TRANSFORMATION

Beginning at 18th level, you can assume the shape of even more powerful creatures. Choose a creature type from among dragons, elementals, and giants. When you use your Form Shift feature, you can morph into a beast, beast-humanoid hybrid, or any creature of the chosen type that you have seen before with a challenge rating as high as your protean level.

Managing Monster Statistics

Many Game Masters consider it inappropriate for players to have access to detailed monster statistics during a tabletop session. Consult with your GM to determine how to best handle the statistics for your protean transformations. In any case, you can help avoid delays by preparing your most common protean form statistics and abilities.

CHAPTER 6: STORMCALLER

A mail-armored gnome parries sword strokes from a trio of human bandits. Seeing the bandit's leader preparing to throw a javelin, the gnome throws his warhammer at the leader. The warhammer strikes the bandit with a deafening thunderclap before returning to the gnome's hand.

A radiant aasimar surrounds herself with winds that buffet and fling a swarm of menacing kobolds. The aasimar uses the opening to regroup with her companions and escape with the kobold's stolen treasures.

Stormcallers command the powers of lightning, thunder, and wind. The most powerful stormcallers can summon deadly storms to defeat their enemies while leaving themselves and their allies untouched.

THUNDER AND LIGHTNING

Many spellcasters learn spells that conjure and control weather. However, stormcallers possess a combination of divine magic and innate power that sets them apart from wizards, clerics, and sorcerers.

Each stormcaller wields a different measure of latent storm magic. Individuals with an affinity for wind and lightning harness their power to conjure and control weather. Stormcallers with an affinity for thunder train in martial combat, and augment their attacks with the power of storms.

DIVINE CONDUITS

A stormcaller might begin their training as the acolyte of a deity who presides over nature or weather. Others undertake magical study, or train as soldiers. Stormcallers learn their true nature when they hear the summons of a deity, or upon encountering another stormcaller who recognizes their gifts.

If a stormcaller reveres a particular deity, they most often take up an adventuring life in response to a command from their deity. The adventuring life also provides opportunities for stormcallers to explore the full potential of their powers while earning fame and fortune.

The Stormcaller – Class Table

Level	Proficiency Bonus	Features
1st	+2	Storm Path, Spellcasting
2nd	+2	Stormbolt
3rd	+2	Stormcaller Path Feature
4th	+2	Ability Score Improvement
5th	+3	Extra Attack
6th	+3	Storm's Blessing
7th	+3	Stormcaller Path Feature
8th	+3	Ability Score Improvement
9th	+4	Lightning Rod
10th	+4	Stormcaller Path Feature
11th	+4	Galvanize
12th	+4	Ability Score Improvement
13th	+5	Stormcaller Path Feature
14th	+5	Storm's Calling
15th	+5	Recharge
16th	+5	Ability Score Improvement
17th	+6	Stormcaller Path Feature
18th	+6	Sheltering Aura
19th	+6	Ability Score Improvement
20th	+6	Stormborn

CREATING A STORMCALLER

When creating your stormcaller, think about how you first discovered your abilities. Did you receive a calling from a deity? If so, do you have a specific divine mission to fulfill? Your inborn power allows you to access storm magic even if you disobey, but incurring the wrath of a deity could place you and your companions in danger.

Some stormcallers never communicate with a deity. Another stormcaller might have taught you the basics of controlling storms, or awakened your powers simply by using their own powers in close proximity to you. Perhaps you discovered your own powers, and turned to adventuring in order to learn the source of your power.

Stormcallers who follow a deity normally share their deity's alignment. Otherwise, the tempestuous power of storms disposes stormcallers towards a chaotic alignment.

QUICK BUILD

You can make a stormcaller quickly by following these suggestions. First, make Strength or Wisdom your highest ability score, depending on whether you want to focus on martial combat or spellcasting. Your next highest ability score should be Constitution. Second, choose the acolyte background.

CLASS FEATURES

As a stormcaller, you gain the following class features.

HIT POINTS

Hit Dice: 1d8 per stormcaller level
Hit Points at 1st Level: 8 + your Constitution modifier
Hit Points at Higher Levels: 1d8 (or 5) + your Constitution modifier per stormcaller level after 1st

PROFICIENCIES

Armor: light armor, shields
Weapons: Simple weapons, mauls, morningstars, warhammers
Tools: None

Saving Throws: Wisdom, Charisma
Skills: Choose two from Arcana, Athletics, History, Insight, Intimidation, Religion, and Survival

EQUIPMENT

You start with the following equipment, in addition to the equipment granted by your background:

- (a) a mace and a shield or (b) a warhammer
- (a) leather armor, or (b) chain mail (if proficient)
- any two simple weapons
- (a) a light crossbow and 20 bolts or (b) five javelins
- (a) a priest's pack or (b) an explorer's pack

SPELLCASTING

The power that infuses you combined with divine magic allows you to cast stormcaller spells. The spells and spell slots available to you depend on your choice of Storm Path, detailed at the end of the class description.

PREPARING AND CASTING SPELLS

The spellcasting tables for each Storm Path show how many spell slots you have to cast your spells of 1st level and higher. To cast one of these spells, you must expend a slot of the spell's level or higher. You regain all expended spell slots when you finish a long rest.

You prepare the list of stormcaller spells that are available for you to cast, choosing from the stormcaller spell list. When you do so, choose a number of stormcaller spells equal to your Wisdom modifier + your stormcaller level (a minimum of one spell). The spells must be of a level for which you have spell slots.

You can change your list of prepared spells when you finish a long rest. Preparing a new list of stormcaller spells requires time spent in prayer and meditation; at least 1 minute per spell level for each spell on your list.

SPELLCASTING ABILITY

Wisdom is your spellcasting ability for your stormcaller spells. The power of your spells comes from your devotion to a deity, and from your understanding of the storm magic that infuses you. You use your Wisdom modifier whenever a stormcaller spell refers to your spellcasting ability. In addition, you use your Wisdom modifier when setting the saving throw DC for a stormcaller spell or class feature and when making an attack roll with one.

Stormcaller save DC =
8 + your proficiency bonus
+ your Wisdom modifier

Spell attack modifier =
your proficiency bonus + your
Wisdom modifier

RITUAL CASTING

You can cast a stormcaller spell as a ritual if that spell has the ritual tag and you have the spell prepared.

SPELLCASTING FOCUS

You can use a holy symbol as a spellcasting focus for your stormcaller spells. In addition, you can use a melee weapon with which you are proficient as a spellcasting focus for your stormcaller spells.

STORM PATH

At 1st level, you choose a path that guides your use of storm magic. Choose the Path of

the Thunderbolt, or the Path of the Whirlwind, both detailed at the end of the class description. Your choice grants you features at 1st level and again at 3rd, 7th, 10th, 13th, and 17th levels.

STORMBOLT

Starting at 2nd level, when you hit a creature with a melee weapon attack, you can expend one stormcaller spell slot to deal thunder and lightning damage to the target, in addition to the weapon's damage.

The extra damage is 1d8 thunder damage + 1d8 lightning damage for a 1st level spell slot, plus 1d8 thunder or lightning damage (your choice) for each spell level higher than 1st, to a maximum of 5d8 extra damage.

If you are proficient with a one-handed melee weapon, that weapon has the thrown property for you, with a normal range of 20 feet, and a long range of 60 feet.

When you hit a creature with a thrown melee weapon, you can expend one stormcaller spell slot to deal thunder and lightning damage to the target, in addition to the weapon's damage. The extra damage is 1d6 thunder damage + 1d6 lightning damage.

ABILITY SCORE IMPROVEMENT

When you reach 4th level, and again at 8th, 12th, 16th, and 19th level, you can increase one ability score of your choice by 2, or you can increase two ability scores of your choice by 1.

If you are using options from *5e Legendary Heroes* to create a heroic character, you can increase an ability score up to a maximum of 30. Otherwise, you can't increase an ability score above 20 using this feature.

EXTRA ATTACK

Beginning at 5th level, you can attack twice, instead of once, whenever you take the Attack action on your turn.

STORM'S BLESSING

At 6th level, the magic that infuses you grants you resistance to lightning and thunder damage.

LIGHTNING ROD

Starting at 9th level, if a spell that deals lightning damage targets a creature other than you within 60 feet of you, you can use your reaction to force the spell to target you instead. If the spell affects an area, you can redirect the spell so that the spell's area of effect includes you. If the spell affects multiple targets of the caster's choice, you can name yourself as one of the spell's targets.

GALVANIZE

By 11th level, you can tap into the magic that infuses you when near death. If you drop to 0 hit points but don't die outright, you can expend a stormcaller spell slot on your turn to gain advantage on death saving throws for 1 minute.

STORM'S CALLING

Beginning at 14th level, you gain immunity to lightning and thunder damage.

RECHARGE

At 15th level, when you cast a spell that deals thunder or lightning damage, or when you are hit with a spell or effect that deals thunder or lightning damage, you can roll a d6. On a 6, you regain one 1st-level stormcaller spell slot.

SHELTERING AURA

Starting at 18th level, friendly creatures within 10 feet of you gain resistance to thunder and lightning damage.

STORMBORN

When you reach 20th level, your mastery of storm magic transforms your body. You gain the following benefits:

- You are immune to disease, poison damage, and the poisoned condition.
- When a creature hits you with a melee attack, you can use your reaction to deal thunder or lightning damage to the attacker (your choice). The damage equals your stormcaller level.
- You can use a bonus action on your turn to disperse your body into a cloud of wind, lightning, and rain that fills a 30-foot diameter sphere. While dispersed, you

can't take any actions, and you can't be targeted by attacks, spells, or other effects. You can end this effect on your turn as a bonus action, appearing at any location you choose within the cloud's area.

STORM PATHS

Your Storm Path reflects the aspect of storms that manifests in your powers. The two most common paths are the Path of the Thunderbolt, and the Path of the Whirlwind.

PATH OF THE THUNDERBOLT

Stormcallers following the Path of the Thunderbolt control the destructive power of thunder. These stormcallers train in the use of magic, and learn combat styles that emphasize crushing blows with bludgeoning weapons.

BONUS PROFICIENCY

When you choose this path at 1st level, you gain proficiency with martial weapons, and medium and heavy armor.

SPELLCASTING

Also starting at 1st level, you gain the ability to cast stormcaller spells.

Cantrips. You learn the *booming blade* cantrip, plus two cantrips of your choice from the stormcaller spell list. You learn an additional cantrip of your choice at 12th level.

Spell Slots. The Thunderbolt Spellcasting table shows how many spell slots you have to cast your spells of 1st level and higher. To cast one of these spells, you must expend a slot of the spell's level or higher. You regain all expended spell slots when you finish a long rest.

THUNDER AFFINITY

Also beginning at 1st level, your connection to thunder enhances your spells and abilities. When you cast a spell of first level or higher that deals thunder damage, the spell deals an additional 1d8 thunder damage.

This damage increases by 1d8 when you reach certain levels in this class: 9th level (2d8), 13th level (3d8), and 17th level (4d8).

Thunderbolt Spellcasting

Stormcaller Level	Cantrips Known	Spell Slots per Spell Level				
		1st	2nd	3rd	4th	5th
1st	3	2	-	-	-	-
2nd	3	3	-	-	-	-
3rd	3	3	-	-	-	-
4th	3	3	-	-	-	-
5th	3	4	2	-	-	-
6th	3	4	2	-	-	-
7th	3	4	3	-	-	-
8th	3	4	3	-	-	-
9th	3	4	3	2	-	-
10th	3	4	3	2	-	-
11th	3	4	3	3	-	-
12th	4	4	3	3	-	-
13th	4	4	3	3	1	-
14th	4	4	3	3	1	-
15th	4	4	3	3	2	-
16th	4	4	3	3	2	-
17th	4	4	3	3	3	1
18th	4	4	3	3	3	1
19th	4	4	3	3	3	2
20th	4	4	3	3	3	2

RESOUNDING SHOUT

At 3rd level, you can use an action on your turn to infuse your voice with resounding thunder. Each creature in a 10-foot radius must make a Constitution saving throw. On a failed save, creatures are deafened for 1 minute. At the end of each of its turns, a creature can make a Constitution saving throw, ending the effect on itself on a success. If a creature fails the saving throw by 5 or more, it is also stunned until the start of your next turn.

In addition, you gain proficiency in the Intimidation skill. If you're already proficient in it, your proficiency bonus is doubled for any check you make with it.

THUNDERCLAP

Starting at 7th level, you can channel storm energy to strike with thunderous force.

As an action, you can make a special melee weapon attack that deals an additional 3d6 thunder damage on a hit. This attack deals double damage to constructs, objects, and structures. To use this feature, you must be wielding a weapon that deals bludgeoning damage, such as a warhammer or maul.

This extra damage increases by 1d6 when you reach certain levels in this class: 9th level (4d6), 11th level (5d6), 13th level (6d6), 15th level (7d6), 17th level (8d6), and 19th level (9d6).

SHATTER BONDS

By 10th level, you have learned to harness thunder to break locks, chains, and barriers. As an action, you use a melee weapon to strike a lock, door, shackle, chain, portal, chest, or the like. The item or passage immediately opens. You can open magical locks and barriers using this feature, provided that they were created by a spell of 7th-level or lower.

Once you use this feature, you cannot use it again until you finish a short or long rest.

SHOCKWAVE

Beginning at 13th level, you can use an action to project a blast of concussive force in a 30-foot cone. Each creature in the cone must make a Constitution saving throw. On a failed save, a creature takes 5d6 thunder damage and is knocked prone. On a successful save, a creature takes half as much damage and isn't knocked prone.

REND THE HEAVENS

At 17th level, you can use an action to call down a bolt of lightning at a point within 120 feet of you. Each creature within 5 feet of that point must make a Dexterity saving throw. A creature takes 7d10 thunder damage and 5d10 lightning damage on a failed save, or half as much damage on a successful one.

You can choose to protect a number of creatures equal to your Wisdom modifier. Protected creatures take no damage from this feature.

Once you use this feature, you cannot use it again until you finish a long rest.

PATH OF THE WHIRLWIND

Stormcallers with a strong connection to wind pursue the Path of the Whirlwind. Stormcallers on this path possess powerful spellcasting abilities, and control violent windstorms.

TEMPEST STRIDE

When you choose this path at 1st level, you gain immunity to bludgeoning damage caused by wind. In addition, wind only moves you if you allow it, and you can use your reaction to determine the direction in which you move.

For example, if a *gust of wind* spell would move you 15 feet further away from a creature, you could instead use your reaction to move 15 feet toward that creature.

SPELLCASTING

Also starting at 1st level, you gain the ability to cast stormcaller spells.

Cantrips. You learn the *gust* cantrip, plus two cantrips of your choice from the stormcaller spell list. You learn additional cantrips of your choice at higher levels, as shown in the Cantrips Known column of the Whirlwind Spellcasting table.

Spell Slots. The Whirlwind Spellcasting table shows how many spell slots you have to cast your spells of 1st level and higher. To cast one of these spells, you must expend a slot of the spell's level or higher. You regain all expended spell slots when you finish a long rest.

SPIRITED STORM

Starting at 3rd level, spells you cast ignore resistance to cold, lightning, and thunder damage.

At 17th level, spells you cast also ignore immunity to cold, lightning, and thunder damage.

WHIRLWIND SHROUD

Beginning at 7th level, you can use an action to surround yourself with a vortex of wind in a 5-foot radius sphere. The sphere spreads around corners. You and creatures within the area have half cover.

The wind keeps fog, smoke, and other gases at bay. Creatures in gaseous form can't pass through it.

The wind immediately stops if you are knocked unconscious, or if you choose to end it on your turn as a bonus action.

WIND STEP

At 10th level, you can cast *levitate* on yourself at will, without expending a spell slot or material components.

If you are surrounded by the wind from your Whirlwind Shroud feature, and while you are outdoors in windy conditions, you don't need to concentrate on this *levitate* to maintain it.

AIR MASTERY

By 13th level, your connection to wind allows you to control the movement of flying creatures. You gain one of the following features of your choice.

Tailwinds. The movement speed of you and friendly creatures within 60 feet of you increases by 10 feet. While flying, hovering, or levitating, you and friendly creatures within 60 feet of you have advantage on Dexterity saving throws.

Hurricane Wind. When a hostile creature flies within 100 feet of you, you can use your reaction to force it to make a Strength saving throw. On a failed save, the creature's flying speed becomes 0, and it is falling. A failing creature takes falling damage as normal upon striking an object or hard surface.

At the end of each of its turns, an affected target can make a Strength saving throw, ending the effect on itself on a success.

SUFFOCATE

Starting at 17th level, you can use an action on your turn to steal the air of one breathing creature within 60 feet of you. The target must make a Constitution saving throw. On a failed save, the target drops to 0 hit points and is dying. On a successful save, the target can't breathe, speak, or perform the verbal components of a spell until the start of its next turn.

Once you successfully drop a creature to 0 hit points using this feature, you cannot use it again until you finish a long rest.

Whirlwind Spellcasting

Stormcaller Level	Cantrips Known	Spell Slots per Spell Level								
		1st	2nd	3rd	4th	5th	6th	7th	8th	9th
1st	3	2	-	-	-	-	-	-	-	-
2nd	3	3	-	-	-	-	-	-	-	-
3rd	3	4	2	-	-	-	-	-	-	-
4th	4	4	3	-	-	-	-	-	-	-
5th	4	4	3	2	-	-	-	-	-	-
6th	4	4	3	3	-	-	-	-	-	-
7th	4	4	3	3	1	-	-	-	-	-
8th	4	4	3	3	2	-	-	-	-	-
9th	4	4	3	3	3	1	-	-	-	-
10th	5	4	3	3	3	2	-	-	-	-
11th	5	4	3	3	3	2	1	-	-	-
12th	5	4	3	3	3	2	1	-	-	-
13th	5	4	3	3	3	2	1	1	-	-
14th	5	4	3	3	3	2	1	1	-	-
15th	5	4	3	3	3	2	1	1	1	-
16th	5	4	3	3	3	2	1	1	1	-
17th	5	4	3	3	3	2	1	1	1	1
18th	5	4	3	3	3	3	1	1	1	1
19th	5	4	3	3	3	3	2	1	1	1
20th	5	4	3	3	3	3	2	2	1	1

STORMCALLER SPELL LIST

Cantrips (0 Level)
Booming Blade
Chill Touch
Frostbite
Gust
Ice Knife
Lightning Lure
Mage Hand
Ray of Frost
Shape Water
Shocking Grasp
Spare the Dying
Thaumaturgy
Thunderclap
True Strike

1st Level
Bless
Catapult
Command
Create or Destroy Water
Detect Magic
Expeditious Retreat
Feather Fall
Fog Cloud
Jump
Protection from Evil and
Good
Sanctuary
Shield
Thunderous Smite
Thunderwave
Unseen Servant

2nd Level
Blur

Dust Devil
Enlarge/Reduce
Gentle Repose
Gust of Wind
Hold Person
Levitate
Magic Weapon
Misty Step
Shatter
Skywrite
Warding Wind

3rd Level
Beacon of Hope
Bestow Curse
Call Lightning
Create Food and Water
Dispel Magic
Lightning Bolt
Protection from Energy
Sleet Storm
Speak with Dead
Stinking Cloud
Tidal Wave
Wall of Water
Water Breathing
Water Walk
Wind Wall

4th Level
Banishment
Conjure Minor Elementals
Control Water
Elemental Bane
Freedom of Movement
Hallucinatory Terrain
Ice Storm
Storm Sphere

Watery Sphere

5th Level
Cloudkill
Commune with Nature
Cone of Cold
Conjure Elemental
Control Winds
Maelstrom
Telekinesis

6th Level
Chain Lightning
Investiture of Ice
Investiture of Wind
Planar Ally
Wall of Ice
Wind Walk
Word of Recall

7th Level
Etherealness
Reverse Gravity
Simulacrum
Symbol
Whirlwind

8th Level
Control Weather
Incendiary Cloud
Power Word Stun
Tsunami

9th Level
Meteor Swarm
Prismatic Wall
Storm of Vengeance
Time Stop

WHAT COMES NEXT?

To fully explore mythic classes, you must use them in an adventure or campaign. Once you have played a few sessions, we would love to hear your stories and feedback.

You can share your Heroic Roleplaying stories with us on Twitter (@heroicrpgs), via email (writers@heroicroleplaying.com), and on our website:

www.heroicroleplaying.com/stories

We encourage you to use mythic classes (and other Heroic 5e content) in your livestreamed and recorded 5e tabletop sessions.

HEROIC CHARACTERS

At your Game Master's discretion, you can choose a mythic class for your heroic character.

Heroic characters possess powers and abilities that mark them as special even among adventurers. Heroic characters often have extraordinary origins, such as a divine parent, famous ancestors, or exposure to extraplanar energies.

Heroic characters who follow standard classes gain additional heroic class options to represent their exceptional abilities. Mythic classes do not gain heroic class options, because mythic classes already wield greater (albeit more specialized) power than standard classes.

However, mythic classes do choose heroic traits as detailed in Chapters 2 and 4 of *5e Legendary Heroes*. **Heroic traits** are talents available only to heroic characters. Heroic traits resemble superpowers, such as flight, telepathy, and elemental mastery.

FURTHER READING

Visit our website (www.heroicroleplaying.com) for the complete line of Heroic 5e titles, including *5e Legendary Heroes*, and *Skyborne*.

Thank you for reading *5e Mythic Classes*. Your support allows us to continue bringing you great 5e content!

APPENDIX A: SHADOW ASSASSIN

When scholars compose treatises on the skills and abilities of adventurers, most subjects fall within neat categories of "class" and "archetype." For example, experts agree that monks who study darkness and stealth adhere to a tradition consistent with the Way of Shadow.

Most texts classify a killer who relies on disguises and poisons as a rogue Assassin. Shadow Assassins eschew disguise in favor of brutal strikes concealed by shadow magic.

Shadow Assassins might belong to monasteries that train adherents to harness ki, or receive training from an assassins' guild. Each path represents a different style of executing similar techniques.

At your Game Master's discretion, you can choose the Shadow Assassin archetype instead of a monastic tradition or roguish archetype when you reach 3rd level in the monk or rogue class.

SHADOW ASSASSIN FEATURES

Monks and rogues who model their training after the archetypal Shadow Assassin master the art of silent, unseen killing.

ASSASSINATE

Starting at 3rd level, you have advantage on attack rolls against any creature that hasn't taken a turn in combat yet. In addition, any hit you score against a creature that is surprised is a critical hit.

SHADOW ARTS

Also beginning when you choose this archetype at 3rd level, you learn to shape darkness and shadow. You have darkvision out to a range of 60 feet. If you already have darkvision, its range increases by 60 feet.

As an action, you can cast *darkness, pass without trace,* or *silence,* without providing material components. You can cast spells using this feature a number of times equal to 1 + your Wisdom modifier (a minimum of twice). You regain all expended uses when you finish a short or long rest.

SHADOW STEP

At 6th level, you gain the ability to step from one shadow to another. When you are in dim light or darkness, as a bonus action you can teleport up to 60 feet to an unoccupied space you can see that is also within dim light or darkness. You then have advantage on the first melee attack you make before the end of your turn.

SHADOW STRIKE

Starting at 9th level, you have learned to attack from the shadows without revealing your position. If you are hidden—both unseen and unheard—the first time you make an attack on your turn, you can choose to impose disadvantage on the attack roll. If the attack hits, you do not give away your position.

CLOAK OF SHADOWS

By 11th level, you have learned to become one with the shadows. When you are in an area of dim light or darkness, you can use your action to become invisible. You remain invisible until you make an attack, cast a spell, or are in an area of bright light.

DEATH STRIKE

Starting at 17th level, you become a master of instant death. When you attack and hit a creature that is surprised, it must make a Constitution saving throw (DC 8 + your Dexterity modifier + your proficiency bonus). On a failed save, double the damage of your attack against the creature.

Design Philosophy: Classes and Toes

Among game designers and in online communities, the concern that a new subclass "steps on the toes" of another class or subclass is sometimes presented as a justification for disallowing a new subclass in 5e. Let's explore the questions: what does it mean for one subclass to step on the toes of another, and why does it matter?

We might say that a new subclass steps on the toes of an existing subclass (or class) if the new subclass has similar or identical abilities to the existing subclass. However, a theme shared by multiple subclasses alone does not qualify. For example, the druid, ranger, Nature Domain cleric, and Oath of Ancients paladin all have nature-based themes, but feature different abilities and encourage diverse character backgrounds.

Classes can even include identical or very similar abilities without toe-stepping. Fighters, paladins, and rangers all have access to a version of the Fighting Style feature. Similarly, both barbarians and monks gain Unarmored Defense.

When most commenters use the phrase "stepping on toes," they seem to mean that the abilities of a new subclass replicate the features of an existing subclass, often in a way that renders the existing subclass obsolete. If an existing class or subclass is found wanting, then the appropriate response is a revision, such as the revised ranger. Creating a new subclass to fix an underperforming subclass only makes the existing subclass redundant without adding anything original for players and Game Masters.

The Shadow Assassin incorporates features already present in the Assassin and Way of Shadow subclasses. For players and Game Masters who fear that the Shadow Assassin steps on the toes of the existing subclasses, consider the Shadow Assassin a revision or variant.

The Shadow Assassin possesses more raw combat potential than its predecessors, because the existing subclasses did not (and it could be argued, were not intended to) fully realize the concept of a shadowy killer. The Assassin's infiltration and disguise abilities, while strongly thematic, have few applications in the context of a group adventure, leaving the Assassin player with little to look forward to from 4th to 16th levels. The monk's Way of Shadow tradition needed significant changes (e.g., darkvision, better offensive abilities) to make the subclass appealing to players.

APPENDIX B: OPTIONAL RULES

This appendix is intended for Game Masters, and details a variety of optional and variant rules. Each rule includes a Suggested Use guide to help you determine if the rule makes sense for your campaign.

Some of the optional rules could influence the character customization choices players make. Explain any optional rules you plan to use at the start of the campaign—don't wait for a relevant scenario to occur.

MARTIAL SPELLCASTING FOCI

If you are proficient with a melee weapon or shield, you can use it as a spellcasting focus for your spells. In addition, you can perform the somatic components of spells even when you have weapons or a shield in one or both hands.

Suggested Use. If you find that players feel compelled to take the War Caster feat, consider this optional rule as a way to encourage them to explore new character customization options.

POWER ATTACK

Before you make an attack with a melee or ranged weapon that you are proficient with, you can choose to take a -5 penalty to the attack roll. If the attack hits, you add +5 to the attack's damage. If you are wielding the weapon with two hands (and the weapon has the two-handed or versatile property), you instead add +10 to the attack's damage.

Suggested Use. This rule opens a portion of the Great Weapon Master and Sharpshooter feats to all players. All weapons now have a chance to deal increased damage in exchange for a penalty to the attack roll.

MONSTER LORE

The multiverse contains many rare, strange, and unnatural creatures. When you encounter a creature for the first time, you can perform an Intelligence check to determine what your character knows about the creature.

Make an Intelligence (Arcana) check to recall information on aberrations, celestials, constructs, elementals, fey, and fiends. Make an Intelligence (Nature) check to recall information on beasts, dragons, giants, humanoids, monstrosities, oozes, and plants. Make an Intelligence (Religion) check to recall information on celestials, fiends, or undead. You can make an Intelligence (History) check to recall information on a famous or legendary creature.

You make the Intelligence check with disadvantage if you are not proficient with the relevant Intelligence skill. You make the Intelligence check with advantage to recall information about creatures commonly found in a region with which you are familiar. Your Game Master might not allow you to make a check at all if you cannot provide an explanation of how your character would have acquired knowledge of an extremely rare creature.

Consult the Monster Lore table for suggestions on the Intelligence check DCs and results on a success. Higher DCs reveal all information gained from lower ability check DCs.

Monster Lore

Intelligence check DC	Result
5	-
10	Common Name; Resistances & Immunities
15	Special Traits; Actions; Senses
20+	Common Spells; Legendary & Lair Actions

Instead of revealing all of the information shown in the Monster Lore table, you can save time by answering only specific questions from the players based on their Intelligence checks.

Suggested Use. The core rules allude to this system without providing detailed guidance to Game Masters. Use this rule in the lower levels (1st-10th level) of play to emphasize the mystery and danger inherent in early monster encounters.

IMPROVED POISON HARVESTING

A character can attempt to harvest poison from a poisonous creature, such as a snake, wyvern, or carrion crawler. The creature must be incapacitated or dead, and the harvesting requires 10 minutes followed by an Intelligence (Nature) check. Proficiency with the poisoner's kit applies to this check if the character doesn't have proficiency in Nature.

Consult the Poison Harvesting table to determine the number of poison doses harvested based on the Intelligence (Nature) check.

Poison Harvesting

Intelligence check DC	Doses
5	0
10	1d4
15	1d6 + 1
20	1d6 + 3
25+	2d6 + 4

On a result of 5 or lower, the harvesting fails, and the character is subjected to the creature's poison.

Suggested Use. A variant of the poison harvesting rules provided in the core 5e books. Some players will go to great lengths to acquire poisoned weapons. Use this optional rule to make poison harvesting easier and more rewarding for players.

If acquiring poison becomes a distraction, you might give the party opportunities to find magic items that deal poison damage, such as the *dagger of venom*, or *staff of the adder*.

PRINCIPLE OF CHARITY

When using a spell, class feature, attack, or ability that requires you to possess certain items or components, you can presume that your character always has the necessary items. Your character is assumed to have taken the time to gather the required items, even if you did not exhaustively roleplay the act of acquiring them.

If a spell or ability (such as the revised ranger's Animal Companion calling, or the *revivify* spell) has a cost in gp, you can subtract the amount in gp from your inventory at the time you use the spell or ability. Your character is assumed to have found, purchased, or otherwise acquired the items beforehand.

Suggested Use. For Game Masters who want a more cinematic campaign that focuses on action and roleplaying, handling mundane tasks "off-screen."

In rhetoric, the principle of charity states that we should interpret the words and actions of others in the most favorable light, assuming that others make statements based on reason. The tabletop principle of charity states that players and Game Masters should presume that the actions of characters make sense in their own universe.

Many players can remember a time when a Game Master told them they could not cast a particular spell, because they did not say in advance that they had the necessary spell components; specifically, players remember how annoyed they felt.

If you plan to enforce strict tracking of ammunition, spell components, inventory, or carrying capacity, tell the players before the campaign begins.

the name of any Contributor unless You have written permission from the Contributor to do so.

12. Inability to Comply: If it is impossible for You to comply with any of the terms of this License with respect to some or all of the Open Game Content due to statute, judicial order, or governmental regulation then You may not Use any Open Game Material so affected.

13. Termination: This License will terminate automatically if You fail to comply with all terms herein and fail to cure such breach within 30 days of becoming aware of the breach. All sublicenses shall survive the termination of this License.

14. Reformation: If any provision of this License is held to be unenforceable, such provision shall be reformed only to the extent necessary to make it enforceable.

15. COPYRIGHT NOTICE

81489676R00033